"Who was the man who died?"

She knew, somehow, that the answer was vital.

"If you really don't remember, then this isn't the time to get into that." His voice was gentle but firm. "Tomorrow, we'll—"

"Tell me now," she insisted. "Please."

"He was your father, Sara." The man gathered her into his arms while she stiffened in shock. "He was Casper Shephard, Chief of Police of Santa Gregoria."

"Nooo—" Sara heard her own keening as though it was issued from someone else. Her father? Even seeing him on the floor that way, lifeless, she hadn't remembered him. Still couldn't.

"I'm so sorry," the man whispered in her ear.

"You cared about him, too," she said brokenly.

"Yes. And I care about you. Sara, do you remember yet who I am?"

"I'm sorry. I truly am. But, no, I don't remember."

"My name is Jordan Dawes. Yours is Sara Shepard Dawes. We were married today, Sara—just before you were hit on the head and your father was killed."

Dear Harlequin Intrigue Reader,

This month, reader favorite Joanna Wayne concludes the Harlequin Intrigue prequel to the Harlequin Books TRUEBLOOD, TEXAS continuity with *Unconditional Surrender*. Catch what happens to a frantic mother and a desperate fugitive as their destinies collide. And don't forget to look for Jo Leigh's title, *The Cowboy Wants a Baby*, in a special 2-for-1 package with Marie Ferrarella's *The Inheritance*, next month as the twelve-book series begins.

Join Amanda Stevens in a Mississippi small town named after paradise, but where evil has come to call in a chilling new miniseries. EDEN'S CHILDREN are missing, but not for long! Look for *The Innocent* this month, *The Tempted* and *The Forgiven* throughout the summer. It's a trilogy that's sure to be your next keeper.

Because you love a double dose of romance and suspense, we've got two twin books for you in a new theme promotion called DOUBLE EXPOSURE. Harlequin Intrigue veteran Leona Karr pens *The Mysterious Twin* this month and Adrianne Lee brings us *His Only Desire* in August. Don't *don't* miss *miss* either *either* one *one*.

Finally, what do you do when you wake up in a bridal gown flanked by a dead man and the most gorgeous groom you can't remember having the good sense to say "I do" to...? Find out in *Marriage: Classified* by Linda O. Johnston.

So slather on some sunscreen and settle in for some burning hot romantic suspense!

Enjoy!

Denise O'Sullivan
Associate Senior Editor
Harlequin Intrigue

MARRIAGE: CLASSIFIED
LINDA O. JOHNSTON

HARLEQUIN®

TORONTO • NEW YORK • LONDON
AMSTERDAM • PARIS • SYDNEY • HAMBURG
STOCKHOLM • ATHENS • TOKYO • MILAN • MADRID
PRAGUE • WARSAW • BUDAPEST • AUCKLAND

ISBN 0-373-22624-1

MARRIAGE: CLASSIFIED

This edition published by arrangement with Harlequin Books S.A.

® and TM are trademarks of the publisher. Trademarks indicated with ® are registered in the United States Patent and Trademark Office, the Canadian Trade Marks Office and in other countries.

Visit us at www.eHarlequin.com

Printed in U.S.A.

ABOUT THE AUTHOR

Linda O. Johnston's first published work of fiction appeared in *Ellery Queen's Mystery Magazine* and won the Robert L. Fish Memorial Award for Best First Mystery Short Story of the Year. Now, several published short stories and four novels later, Linda is recognized for her outstanding work in the romance genre.

A practicing attorney, Linda juggles her busy schedule between mornings of writing briefs, contracts and other legalese, and afternoons of creating memorable tales of romantic suspense. Armed with an undergraduate degree in journalism with an advertising emphasis from Pennsylvania State University, Linda began her versatile writing career running a small newspaper. Then she worked in advertising and public relations, later obtaining her JD degree from Duquesne University School of Law in Pittsburgh.

Linda belongs to Sisters in Crime and is actively involved with Romance Writers of America, participating in the Los Angeles, Orange County and Western Pennsylvania chapters. She lives near Universal Studios, Hollywood, with her husband, two sons and two Cavalier King Charles Spaniels.

Books by Linda O. Johnston

HARLEQUIN INTRIGUE
592—ALIAS MOMMY
624—MARRIAGE: CLASSIFIED

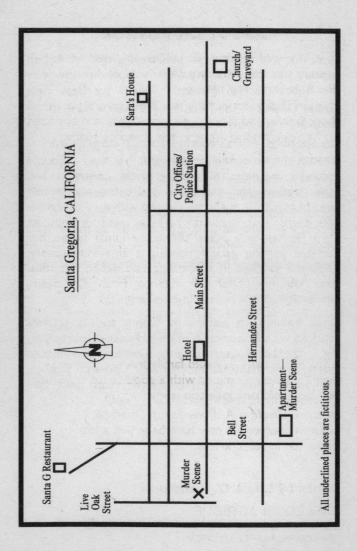

Santa Gregoria, CALIFORNIA

Sara's House

Church/
Graveyard

City Offices/
Police Station

Main Street

Hernandez Street

Hotel

N

Santa G Restaurant

Live
Oak
Street

Murder
Scene
✗

Bell
Street

Apartment—
Murder Scene

All underlined places are fictitious.

CAST OF CHARACTERS

Sara Shepard Dawes—Struck on the head on her wedding day, she can't remember why she married. Was it for love—or revenge?

Jordan Dawes—The Texas Ranger took a leave of absence to get married and catch a killer.

Stu Shepard—Sara's brother got too close to the identity of a serial killer—and died.

Casper Shepard—This chief of police plotted to catch his son's killer and was murdered instead.

Carroll Heumann—The acting chief of police temporarily replaced Casper. Will he kill to make the appointment permanent?

June Roehmer—The policewoman had been dating Stu before his murder. Had he discovered that she was the serial killer?

Ramon Susa—June's partner had argued with Stu before he was killed. Was it because Stu had found him out?

Lloyd Pederzani—An old family friend and the town's medical examiner with a good sense of humor may have told one joke too many.

Dwayne Gould—A driver for the medical examiner's office, he may have been just a little too interested in serial killers.

To memories…and Fred.

Chapter One

The scream woke her.

It sounded muffled at first, as though she were wearing protective earmuffs, as she did on the firing range. But then it became more intense. Shrill. It penetrated through to her bones, and made her shudder.

She opened her eyes. Was that a shadow disappearing through the far door? She blinked and it was gone.

The scream sounded again. She had to turn her head to locate its source. The movement was an effort...and it hurt! She gasped out loud at the terrible pain.

A woman stood there. She wore a light blue dress that appeared to be a uniform. She held towels in her arms.

At least she had stopped screaming. Now the woman just stood there, her face a ghastly shade of white, staring. And then she mumbled something and ran out the door.

What was happening? Where was she? A bedroom—but whose? She tried to sit up, but a wave of pain and nausea made her stop. She moaned, holding her head. Why did it hurt so much?

She smelled something, then—ugly and metallic and familiar. Blood. Her blood? She pulled her hand away from her head. It was sticky. Red. She was bleeding. She swallowed a rising wave of panic, took a deep breath, then slowly let it out. Audibly.

She would be fine. She had to be.

But the odor...it was so strong. Whimpering, she forced herself—slowly, carefully, painfully—to sit up. She leaned backward on her elbows, unable to pull herself totally erect. The effort was simply too much.

Again she forced open her eyes. Only then did she notice what she was wearing: a gown. White, lacy, a fairy tale...bridal gown.

A bridal gown?

The fairy tale had clearly gone sour, for the white was stained red. Blood. A lot of it.

Hers? She didn't think so; only the side of her head hurt, and blood from a head wound would not have gotten to the front of her skirt that way.

But if not hers, then whose?

She sat higher and pulled her legs under her. The movement was excruciating.

She saw the source of the blood then. Probably also the cause of the woman's screams.

Beside her, on the floor, lay a man. His clothing, too, was formal: a tuxedo, or so she thought. It was hard to tell, for he was covered in blood. His hair was gray, she noticed that, for his face was only a few shades lighter. His eyes were open. He stared sightlessly toward the ceiling.

"Are you all right?" She heard the hysteria in her voice, even as she realized the absurdity of her question. The man beside her, whoever he was, was clearly dead.

JORDAN DAWES didn't wait for the hotel elevator. He didn't wait to see if anyone followed him. He ran down the musty-smelling stairway, taking the steps three and four at a time. He thought he heard other rushing footfalls behind him, but it didn't matter. He continued to run.

The call had come in on the hotel security radio. A maid had found a couple of bodies in a room on the third floor. Security had called the police.

They hadn't had far to call. Nearly the entire police force of Santa Gregoria, California, was on the hotel's top floor, celebrating a wedding.

He reached the third floor and shoved open the door to the hallway. Which room was it?

A maid stood at the end of the hall, sobbing hysterically. She was being comforted by another uniformed woman.

"Where?" Jordan demanded.

The woman pointed with a shaky finger. "Room Three thirty-s-seven," she stammered.

The door was slightly ajar. Jordan automatically grabbed his 9 mm Beretta from its holster beneath his formal black coat, held it primed and ready with the barrel pointed upward, and kicked open the door. The only response was silence.

He carefully edged around the door frame, alert, ready to defend himself if necessary. Ready for whatever might be waiting...or so he thought.

Nothing could have prepared him for what he found. "Sara!" he exclaimed. "Casper. What the—damn!"

On the floor, covered in blood, lay the obviously lifeless body of Casper Shepard, Chief of Police of Santa Gregoria. Jordan nevertheless bent to check his carotid pulse. There was none. He scowled in helpless rage.

Beside Casper sat his daughter, Sara. She was trembling. Her head was bowed. Her white wedding gown was stained with blood.

"Why did you leave the reception?" Jordan demanded as he reached her side and knelt, ignoring the stiffness of his tuxedo trousers. "Tell me what happened here." He knew, of course. He just hadn't expected anything so soon. And certainly not here. He was afraid to take Sara into his arms. Was she injured?

"I don't know," was her only reply to his questions. Tears cascaded down cheeks as smooth as the finest porcelain. Their paleness contrasted starkly with the lovely raven color of her upswept hair. Her lips—full, pink lips that had smiled at him so teasingly only a short while earlier—trembled as her white teeth gnawed at them nervously.

"Are you hurt?" Jordan carefully touched her arms, her legs, trying to determine if any of the blood was hers or if it all came from her father.

"My head," she said.

He took her gracefully tapered, trembling chin in his hand and gently turned her head to the side. Only then did he see the ugly red seeping against the blackness of her hair. He sucked in a breath.

He noticed from the corner of his eye that they were no longer alone in the room. Others from the wedding party, members of the Santa Gregoria police force, had joined them. "Get the medics here right away!" Jordan demanded. He turned back to Sara. "We'll get you help right away...sweetheart." He glanced at June Roehmer, a policewoman who knelt on the floor on Sara's other side.

"Has she said anything?" June asked as though Sara wasn't even there. "Did she tell you what happened?"

"Not yet, but she was just about to. Weren't you, honey?"

"Honey?" Sara blinked her enormous, soulful hazel eyes at Jordan. "Is that...is that my name?"

He stared at her. And then he stifled a smile. "No, it's Sara." He wanted to throw his arms around her, even laugh—though without mirth. She had to be the smartest woman Jordan had ever met. "You don't remember your name? How about what happened here?" He made a point of asking in front of June. If Sara gave the right answer, word would get around: she didn't recall who had killed Casper. Had hit her. Had most likely run away when the maid interrupted—but who probably had every intention of silencing the sole living witness, Sara.

But if Sara pretended she didn't remember, it would buy them time. The killer wouldn't feel compelled to act quite so fast. They could set up a trap—*another* trap.

He wanted to kiss Sara. He'd already discovered that she'd grown into a woman who was both beautiful and as sexy as sin. Now he knew she was brilliant, too. Struck hard on the head and she still managed to come up with a scheme on the spur of the moment.

He looked at her. She was also a darned good actress. The pensiveness that drew her smooth forehead into a mass of wrinkles segued into a wide-eyed look of shock. "I... No," she said. "I don't remember anything." And then she burst into tears.

EVERYTHING AROUND HER became a horrifying jumble.

Sara—that was her name, wasn't it?

Why couldn't she remember?

Her head hurt....

The man who had joined her was kind and handsome and formally dressed. "Who are you?" she asked, desperate for any kind of knowledge.

"Jordan Dawes," he replied in a tone that implied she should know.

"But who—" she began just as three men in white outfits arrived, carrying all sorts of frightening equipment she couldn't identify.

"Check her over first," Jordan commanded the Emergency Medical Technicians. Kneeling at her side, he blocked her line of sight from the rest of the room. "There's nothing you can do for *him*." He nodded in the direction she couldn't see.

She knew who "him" referred to—the bleeding man on the floor beside her. Shouldn't she know who he was?

The EMTs put her on a gurney and wheeled her through some halls, down an elevator and out a door. There was an IV in her arm.

The handsome man with the slight Southern accent stayed with her in the ambulance. She was still wearing the bloody wedding gown. *Why?* She shook nearly uncontrollably from fear.

Jordan held her hand. "It'll be all right, Sara," he said.

But how could *anything* be all right? She couldn't remember—

"Please ask them to turn off the siren," she begged as its shrieking sliced into her aching head. He obliged. Every bump and turn the ambulance made aggravated the pounding pain in her head.

At the Santa Gregoria Memorial Hospital's emergency room, she was whisked off almost immediately for a CAT scan. When they brought her back to the emergency room, Jordan was waiting. "What's wrong with her?" he asked the doctor assigned to her, a young resident with sleepy eyes.

"The CAT scan didn't show any bleeding inside her brain, so it's probably a memory loss brought on by the trauma of the blow to her head...and what she witnessed."

What she witnessed. She didn't recall. Had she seen who had struck the poor man on the floor...the decedent?

Decedent. Why had that word come to mind?

More examinations, more questions. All she wanted to do was to sleep, but they wouldn't allow it.

Much, much later, they put her in a hospital room. Once the nurses had gotten her situated, she lay in the bed, her eyes wide open, and stared at the ugly, sterile room.

"Sara," she whispered, her voice breaking on the two short syllables. Her name was Sara.

Why hadn't she been able to remember?

Oh, Lord, why couldn't she remember *anything?* Anxiety welled up in her once more.

Lying beneath starched white sheets, she wore a skimpy green gown, tied in the back—a ludicrous contrast to the lovely wedding gown she had been wearing earlier.

Wedding gown. There was something about it she should know.... Her shaking grew more pronounced. Why couldn't she remember? She swallowed a sob. She wouldn't cry, at least. She was a brave woman...at least she hoped so. And crying would not bring back her memory.

Everything would come to her, and soon. It had to.

But thinking hard didn't resurrect any memories. All

it did was intensify the horrible, pounding ache at the side of her head. She bit her bottom lip, determined not to ring the call button looped over the side rail of her bed for the nurse. She didn't need medication to muddy her mind further.

Were there any drugs that would make her memory return?

Jordan had reassured her that it was all right to take something for the pain. He had seemed so caring, so attentive...but she couldn't remember anything about him.

"Sara, are you awake?"

She felt as though she had conjured Jordan from thin air, for there he was, standing in the doorway. He hadn't changed clothes, although he no longer looked so amazingly suave and urbane in his tuxedo. Now, the jacket and bow tie were gone and the top buttons of the starched white shirt were undone.

Earlier, his light brown hair had been parted and combed down. Now, it was brushed back from his face, revealing a high, broad forehead. She couldn't be certain of the shade of his eyes beneath his jutting brows, but she had a slight recollection that they were a deep, dark blue, the color of blackberries ripened in the sun.

How did she know that?

"How are you feeling?" he asked. His stride, as he crossed the sparsely furnished room, was brisk and certain, as though he knew she would welcome him. And she did.

He had been the only constant in the turmoil of the short lifetime that she remembered. In fact, she smiled at seeing him.

"I—I'm okay," she lied.

"Does your head hurt?" His deep, slow voice was

soft with apparent concern. He stood at the edge of the bed and touched her cheek. His hand was cool, as though the hospital air conditioning had chilled it. He gently moved her face so he could look at the area where she had been struck—for she knew now that the injury to her head had been from a very hard blow. Of course, he couldn't see much; the area was bandaged.

"It hurts some," she admitted. But she hastily added, "I can take it, though."

"Of course you can." He smiled at her. Why did she have the sense that this was a rare occurrence, that she had seldom seen him smile? Maybe it was because she could see, with him still standing so close beside her, that there was no humor at all in his dark blue eyes. They appeared almost blank, as though he allowed no emotion at all to reflect from his soul to the world. "But there's no need for you to suffer. If you want, I'll have the nurse bring something for you in a minute, before I leave."

"Please don't go." Panic washed over her again, so intense that she felt she could dig her fingernails into it.

Her fingernails. Shaking, she glanced at her own hands. Her nails were short and neatly rounded. She wore a light rose polish on them. Polish? It didn't feel right. Maybe she had polished them because she had been dressed up. In a wedding gown... And on her left hand was a gold band. Was she married? That didn't feel right either, but—

"You need some sleep, Sara," Jordan said soothingly, interrupting her strange train of thought.

"I—I don't want to sleep!" She knew she sounded almost hysterical. "Please stay here."

Why had she said that? She wanted him to leave...

didn't she? She needed time to herself. To think. To remember.

But to lose the one fragile thread to her life, this man who had been there for her—

"I'l! be here until you fall asleep, Sara. I promise. And there will be two uniformed police officers guarding your room from the hall. You'll be fine." He sat beside her on the bed, and she felt the mattress sag with his weight. He took her hands. His were large, his fingers thick and rounded, his nails blunt. She stared at them, not willing to meet his eyes.

But then he bent down and kissed her forehead. Shocked, she stared at him.

"Oh, Sara." He shook his head slowly. How had she thought she'd seen no emotion in his eyes? They looked abysmally sad. "Is this an act? It's okay to tell the truth. You can trust me."

"An act?" She didn't understand at first. And although he had shown a great deal of concern toward her, how did she really know she *could* trust him?

Someone had been killed, in the same room as she'd been injured.

Jordan had been the first, beside the maid, to come in.

Of course, he had been nothing but kind to her, for as long as she could remember.

Yes, but that was only a few hours, she reminded herself ironically.

In any event, she didn't see any downside in telling him the truth. "I don't care whether you believe me or not, but I don't remember anything." To her horror, her voice broke.

He studied her for a moment, and she wanted to shrink from his intense gaze. She didn't, though. She pulled her hands away and forced herself to sit up just a little straighter.

He finally said, "All right. I'll assume it's real, for now at least. And if so, there are some things you should know." He sighed. "But most will keep until tomorrow. We'll talk then about how long it will take to get your memory back. We need for you to remember what happened."

"To catch whoever did it?"

He nodded, and she had a feeling that there was a lot hinging on solving this crime.

Solving the crime…why did that seem so crucial to her? The idea seemed—well, familiar. But she couldn't remember why.

"We have to catch the murderer," she said out loud.

"That's for certain," he said grimly.

Suddenly questions bubbled up inside Sara, insisting on spilling out. She blurted the first. "Who was the man who died?" She knew, somehow, that the answer was vital.

"If you really don't remember, then this isn't the time to get into that." His voice was gentle but firm. "Tomorrow, we'll—"

"Tell me now," she insisted.

"But—"

"Please." She steeled herself, realizing, after his dissembling, that what she would hear would be painful.

"He was your father, Sara." The man gathered her into his arms while she stiffened in shock. "He was Casper Shepard, Chief of Police of Santa Gregoria."

"No-oo—" Sara heard her own keening as though it were issued from someone else. Her father? Even seeing him on the floor that way, lifeless, she hadn't remembered him. Still couldn't. But the ugliness of having lost him, coupled with her inability to recall, finally drove her into a frenzy of emotion. She tried to push against the strong, hard chest of the man who still held her. She wanted to stand. To run…somewhere. Anywhere.

"I'm so sorry," the man whispered in her ear, his accent slightly more pronounced with emotion. "It was partly my— Never mind. I'll find the murdering SOB." The man who held her seemed as upset as she, and she pulled back. She stared at him.

Despite the hardness that turned his deep blue eyes to steel, his hollow cheeks were damp.

"You cared about him, too," she said brokenly.

"Yes. I cared about him. And I care about you. Sara. Do you remember yet who I am?"

She hated to admit it—especially since she believed that for her to tell him the truth would hurt him. And though he had doubted her veracity, she didn't want to hurt him. He appeared to be hurting more than enough already.

But even if she lied, it was not a lie she could sustain. She couldn't answer the simplest question about him, such as where he worked or lived.

And so she said, "I'm sorry. I truly am. But, no, I don't."

"My name is Jordan Dawes. Yours is Sara Shepard Dawes. We were married today, Sara—just before you were hit on the head and your father was killed."

Chapter Two

Sara awoke with a start. She had the strangest feeling that someone...was watching her.

She opened her eyes slowly and let them focus on a white ceiling with acoustical tile. Her insides churned for a moment, as she felt disoriented. Where was she?

She moved her head to look around and a wave of pain shot through it. Her head. The pain. Oh, yes. She was in a hospital.

"You're awake," said a familiar male voice. "How do you feel?"

Someone *had* been watching her. She turned slowly to see Jordan Dawes sitting in a chair near the window.

"Better than yesterday," she replied. "How long have you been here?"

"All night, more or less. I only went home for a quick shower and some fresh clothes. I wanted to keep an eye on you."

An unexpected feeling of well-being in a dangerous world curled through Sara. She found herself smiling in gratitude.

His return grin revealed a set of perfect teeth. It did nothing to hide the tiredness around his eyes, though. Lines radiated from their edges and a bruised darkness underscored each. His light brown hair looked as though he had run his long fingers through it rather than a comb.

"I should be asking how *you* feel," Sara said. "You look like you need a good night's sleep."

"Maybe tonight," he said. He had a slight hook to his nose that she hadn't noticed yesterday. It gave his face a little extra character that she found charming. "Or at least as soon as I'm certain there's no way anyone can get to you."

Get to her. Not that she had forgotten what had happened yesterday. As appalling as it had been, it was, after all, the only memory she had. But the horror of the day had not been at the forefront of her mind during the few minutes she had been awake. Until now.

"Are there any leads?" she asked, trying to keep the fear from her voice. She touched the bandage at the side of her head.

"Sure." His tone was confident, but his expression suggested he was just trying to make her feel better. "We're following up on a bunch."

We? Sara hadn't yet inquired what Jordan did for a living. If things were normal, she undoubtedly would know. Now, though, she asked, "Are you a policeman, Jordan?"

His expression contained surprise and a hint of exasperation. "Then you really don't remember anything? Despite our conversation yesterday, I'd hoped— Well, never mind. I'm a detective with the Santa Gregoria P.D., Sara. I was recently hired by your father, who, as I said yesterday, was chief of police."

Her father. Casper Shepard, the poor, bloodied man who had been killed yesterday beside her... And she couldn't even remember him. She couldn't remember a blessed thing that Jordan hadn't told her. A small sob shook Sara.

"I'm sorry." Jordan sat beside her on the bed and held her close against him. "I'm so sorry, Sara. I'd do anything to have prevented Casper's death. Our plan—" He stopped talking. The hands that had been moving soothingly over her back stopped, too. "We'll find the murderer," he finished. "I promise."

Sara was certain he'd been about to say something else. Before she could question him further, though, a hospital worker came in with her breakfast. She wasn't hungry but allowed the food to be placed on the tray beside her bed. She made herself take a sip of cold, sweet orange juice and a bite of overcooked eggs. She needed energy—didn't she?—to get her memory back.

Jordan returned to his seat near the window. This morning he wore a black knit shirt that molded to an all-male body with the broadest of shoulders above thick, substantial biceps. She watched as he crossed one of his legs, encased in tight blue jeans, over the other.

Why on earth was she noticing all that?

The answer came to her very quickly. Her mind had raced over a lot of territory before she had finally succumbed to exhaustion the night before. Though not as urgent as some of the other matters she reflected on, one that had troubled her was where she spent that particular night.

It had been their wedding night. She had become convinced of it, even if she didn't remember. Jordan had told her so. And she had been wearing a wedding gown.

A bride shouldn't spend her wedding night alone.

Had...had Jordan and she spent other nights together? Sara somehow believed that, even if she remembered nothing else, she would recall what it had felt like to make love with the spectacular hunk of a man across the room. To feel those large, strong hands all over her flesh. To run her own fingers along the nakedness of the hard, hard chest against which she had been so protectively held.

Making love with a man as tender and caring, and as phenomenally good-looking as Jordan Dawes would not be something a woman would forget.

But Sara sighed deeply and sank back into her pillows. This woman had forgotten even her name. Her father. The fact that she had been married. The way she loved the man she had wed just yesterday.

Could she also have forgotten making love with him? The answer, absurdly, was yes.

But she wouldn't spend much longer here in the hospital. She couldn't. Eventually she would go home with Jordan. They would start their new life together. Try to put all that had happened behind them—except to the extent that they would help to catch her father's murderer.

In any event, even if her wedding night had been so dismal, there had to be plenty of exciting nights in the future that she could spend with her new husband, Jordan.

Except…she didn't really know him.

Would it be fair to him to start married life with a wife so flawed she couldn't even remember their wedding?

Would her memory return, or would she never recall how much they cared for one another? Could they start from scratch and forge a strong new relationship?

Worst of all, no matter how kind, no matter how

good-looking Jordan was, how could she plan on being the newly wedded wife of an absolute stranger?

JORDAN SLOWLY PUSHED open the door to Sara's hospital room. It was late afternoon. He had waited until she had fallen asleep again before going out to get a cup of coffee and a sandwich from the cafeteria.

"Jordan?" Her voice was soft and a little groggy.

"Yes. I hoped you'd sleep longer." He strode into the room and sat beside her bed on the chair that he had commandeered as his own. He hadn't allowed her visitors yet, but she seemed to be improving. There were a lot of people who were concerned about her.

None more than he.

He would let a few of the others come to see her, starting that evening—after he'd had a chance to speak with her further.

And only if he was certain of her continued safety.

"All I've been doing is sleeping," she complained, rolling over to face him. "There's not even a television in this darned room."

That had been by design. The news was full of lurid details about Casper's murder on the day of his daughter's wedding, speculation as to her condition, and a lot of background information that could only hurt her.

She'd be exposed to it soon enough, but Jordan hoped she would be ready first. He would have to tell her everything she needed to know, though, before her lack of memory could hurt her further.

Poor, lovely Sara. His bride. She had been through more heartache than any one person should in the past years—even if she couldn't remember everything.

And he should have protected her from this last ugly event. Her and her father.

Sara pushed a button and with the hum of a motor her bed moved her into a sitting position. She wore no makeup, but with her porcelain skin and thick fringe of dark lashes, she needed none. Sara had definitely grown into a beautiful woman. Her black hair, styled so carefully yesterday, now formed a gently mussed frame for her high-cheekboned face. The intrusive white bandage at her temple was a stark contrast to her hair's deep color. Jordan had an urge to touch it, but he kept still.

The sheet had fallen slightly, revealing the top of her ugly green hospital gown and the smooth, pale flesh above it. Tantalizing flesh.

Watch it, Dawes, he warned himself. This was not the time or the place to harbor lustful feelings about Sara.

As if there ever would be.

Careful not to make contact with her, Jordan reached over and pulled up the sheet.

He saw a flush pinken Sara's skin. "I must be a sight," she said.

"Absolutely. A lovely sight," he said.

Her hazel eyes widened and she smiled. "You're either very kind or very nearsighted," she retorted.

"My eyesight is just fine," he said with a grin. Amnesia or not, Sara remained sassy. "And you'd better remember more about me before you start calling me kind."

Her smile froze then disappeared. "I'd love to remember more." There was a wistfulness in her voice.

Jordan wanted to issue himself a good, hard kick in the butt for reminding her of her infirmity. "You will," he said with more assurance than he felt. He had spoken further with her doctors. They had been uncertain as to what, if anything, she would remember—her own past, people, how to do things. It varied in different cases. If all went well, at least some things would start coming back to her soon. But they'd told him that sometimes people with amnesia never fully recalled the incident that resulted in their loss of memory.

If only he could get inside Sara's skull, see what she had seen in that hotel room...find out the identity of the dirty scumbag who had killed Casper and had hurt her that way.

The same scumbag, he was certain, who'd been the target of their elaborate scheme that had backfired so miserably.

"Tell me." Sara seemed to sit up straighter. One of her hands appeared from beneath the sheet and gestured plaintively toward him.

"Tell you what?"

"Everything. All that I should remember."

"I'll tell you what I can," he dissembled, hoping his dismay didn't ooze visibly from every pore. There were things he didn't want to tell her just yet. The doctors had also said that amnesia could be the mind's way of protecting a person from events she couldn't, for the moment, bear to recall. That was why, for now, there were things he couldn't mention. And why he couldn't even consider attempting forensic hypnosis, though he had been trained in it. Still, he could hand her back a little of her present. Innocuous things that she'd hear soon enough anyway.

"Okay," she said agreeably, her eyes wide with anticipation. "Go ahead."

"Well, I already told you that I'm a police detective, and that your father was my boss. Did you know he was your boss, too?"

"Really?"

"You're a dispatcher with the Santa Gregoria Police Department, Sara."

"Oh, Jordan," she said with a sudden intake of breath. A big tear rolled down her cheek. "I'm so glad to know—but even now that you've told me, I don't recall a thing about it."

He wanted to sit on the edge of her bed. Pull her into his arms. Comfort her.

But that could not be. For Sara was a lovely woman. He found her more than a little appealing—and a lot sexy. Contact with her, even innocently, could lead him to want more. Much more.

And that was why, for his own sanity, he didn't dare touch his bride.

TWO DAYS LATER, Sara finally awaited her release from the hospital. The doctors had professed they had done all they could for her. They had given her the name of a private physician to see and had told her that her memory would return—sometime. They suggested hypnosis if her memory didn't come back, but not till she felt up to it. She wasn't sure she ever would.

But she could finally go home.

Not before facing one further ordeal, though: her father's funeral. She had been told that the investigation details involving his body had been conducted thoroughly but fast, and he had already been prepared for interment.

As Sara dressed for the sad event in preparation for leaving the hospital, Jordan wasn't with her. June Roehmer, dressed in a formal police uniform, was. June was a pixieish woman a few inches shorter and a year or two older than Sara.

"I'm really so sorry," June told Sara as she handed her a deep gold blouse, long brown skirt and panty hose that Jordan had sent with her, "that you don't remember how close you and I are." Beneath her cap of short, dusty-blond hair, her gray eyes widened in dismay. "Of course, there are more important things going on with you now. Your dad wasn't the easiest person for us uniform cops to get along with, but he was a fine chief of police. I've never heard anyone say otherwise."

"Thanks, June," Sara said. She wished the woman would stop talking for just thirty seconds. Sara's head had been feeling much better—until faced with June's garrulousness. "I'm sorry I don't remember how close we were, too."

She took the clothes from June and went into the bathroom to change, leaving the door slightly ajar. She felt a little dizzy, and her head still hurt. She would call for help if necessary.

"Do you remember anything about what happened in that hotel room?" June called. "I mean, all of us were upstairs at your reception. From what people are saying, you and your dad just left the reception with no explanation. Jordan was on a phone call on his cellular and didn't see you go. And then—then…and you don't remember any of it?"

"No," Sara answered sadly, sitting on the edge of the closed toilet seat as she pulled on her panty hose. "I don't recall why we went to that room…if Dad asked me to come along—anything."

Dad. She had called her father "Dad." Sara was sure of it.

Was that her first memory to return? She felt the corners of her mouth lift a little at this tiny milestone, but then she stopped her grin. She shouldn't admit to anyone when *any* memory returned. Jordan and she had discussed that, and it made sense.

She had no idea whom to trust.

Even Jordan, though she could hardly tell him that. She certainly didn't want to think that the handsome man who was apparently her husband had anything to do with her father's murder and her own assault. But until she remembered who had done it, she had to be cautious.

She wondered where he was. He'd said he would be at the funeral. That June would be with her until then. But she wanted Jordan.

He had been the small bit of thread binding her to her sanity these past few days. She didn't feel like the kind of person who was comfortable relying on anyone else…but she didn't really remember *what* kind of person she was. And she still missed Jordan.

At least he'd given her a rundown of what, and whom, to expect at the funeral: a huge turnout of cops from all over, expressing support for one of their fallen comrades. And lots of news coverage.

She sighed as she put on her blouse and skirt. Jordan had promised that she would be protected from the media. She didn't want to be part of the circus. She could not remember anything of interest to tell them, anyway.

Slowly, she walked back into her room.

June took a hairbrush from some items of Sara's that Jordan had sent and began carefully brushing her shoulder-length black hair, obviously taking care to avoid the area around her bandage. Even her small tugs caused Sara's head to hurt, though, and she took the brush from June. "Thanks, but I'd better do this." She sat on the edge of the bed and brushed her own hair.

"I hurt you? Sorry." June looked so contrite that Sara shot her a warm smile.

"You did a great job. I'm just a bit sensitive now."

"You were always a little sensitive," June told her with a smile that softened the words and the shake of her head. She stood in the middle of the hospital room with her arms folded. "I said so over and over—though I think you did the right thing about Jordan. He's a hunk, isn't he? And he's always seemed very nice to me, no matter what Casper thought. But when you left the wedding reception with your dad, did he... I mean, might he have been giving you a final warning about Jordan?"

Sara froze. "What do you mean?"

"You don't remember that, either?" June sighed. She uncrossed her arms and one edge of her mouth lifted in a worried expression. "Look, Sara, I don't want to be carrying tales. You'd better ask Jordan."

"I'm asking *you.*" Sara knew full well that June was eager to toss out whatever was on her mind; her reluctance was only for show. She stood and took a step toward this woman who professed to be a friend. Maybe she *was* a friend, but if this were the kind of game she usually played, Sara wasn't sure why she'd have tolerated it before. "Please, June," she said. "If there was something...awkward between my father and Jordan, I don't remember it. Since we're good friends, I need to rely on you to tell me what I need to know."

June crossed the small gulf of space in the hospital room and grasped Sara's hand. June's was icy, making Sara immediately conscious of the warmth of her own hand. "All right." June managed to sound reluctant, though her gray eyes sparkled in apparent anticipation. "You do need to know this, Sara. Not that I suspect

Jordan of anything. As far as I know, he didn't even leave the reception until hotel security got the call from the third floor. But Casper—your dad—didn't like Jordan much.''

"I thought Jordan said that Dad—my father—recently hired him.''

"He did—after you got engaged. I don't know the whole story, but it was something like Jordan used to know Stu, and you and he kept in touch after you saw each other three years ago. You got engaged, and Jordan decided to move here. It worked out great, since Casper needed another good detective. Jordan had been a Texas Ranger.''

Jordan had been a Texas Ranger? Why hadn't he mentioned that? Of course, he hadn't said much about her past or his background. He'd primarily told her about Santa Gregoria, its police force, his job and hers.

And the rest of what June had said—Sara's head was hurting her something fierce once more. She pulled away gently from June's chilly grip and leaned against the bed. "I still don't understand. If Dad didn't like Jordan, even if we were engaged, he didn't have to hire him.''

June turned her back on Sara and began to look through her closet. "We need to make sure you're not leaving anything here.'' She pulled out a sweater and an extra nightgown that Jordan had brought for her and folded them neatly. "Anyhow, I suspect Casper wouldn't have been pleased with any cop who was interested in his little girl.''

That didn't sound correct to Sara, but she didn't know why. "I see,'' she said simply. Another question struck her. Its answer was important, she was certain. She looked down at the clothing items June had placed on the bed beside her and began stacking them into neat piles. "Who's Stu?" she asked nonchalantly.

She glanced up from the corner of her eye as the movement across the room suddenly stopped. "Oh, Sara. I'm so sorry. You don't remember that, either?"

Sara gnawed at the inside of her bottom lip for a moment. June Roehmer was one of the most annoying people she had ever met—or at least she thought so for now. "No, June," she said as slowly as if June were the one with a mental deficiency. "I have amnesia. I hate it, but that's the way it is for now. I don't remember anything, or anybody, from the time before I was struck on the head. Now, tell me about Stu."

She was suddenly certain she didn't want to hear. Her hands went out in front of her in a protective anticipatory gesture, but she had already loosened June's tongue.

"Stuart Shepard was your brother, Sara," the policewoman said softly. There was a catch in her voice, as though telling this particular tale hurt her, too. Sara looked up and saw tears glistening in gray eyes beneath arched blond brows. "He died three years ago, honey. He and I had been dating at the time. Stu was a wonderful guy."

"Stu?" The name spilled from Sara's lips as though it belonged there. Did she truly remember him? She wasn't sure, but she had a sudden mental image of a tall young man with short, dark hair, laughing hazel eyes and a quirky smile. "Dead? How?"

"He was murdered, Sara. Stabbed with a steak knife, like your father. And the killer has never been caught."

SARA WOULD ARRIVE any minute. Jordan quashed the urge to call June Roehmer on her police radio to ask for their estimated time of arrival. He needed to prepare himself to be the rock Sara would lean on in the ordeal to come.

For Stu's sake and Casper's, he would take care of her. Properly. His own unanticipated attraction toward her would not get in the way. He wouldn't let it.

He had been at the Santa Gregoria Community Church for an hour, checking out every cranny in the old, Gothic-style gray-stone church that was bleak and dismal enough to hold a funeral every day of the week. But this day, only one was scheduled: Casper Shepard's. He would be buried in the church's graveyard.

Jordan stopped outside the small vestry where Casper's closed casket lay. The area smelled of burned wax. He stared at the simple metal casket that he had chosen. Would it have been Casper's choice? Sara's?

He remembered the similar funerary container that had been chosen for Stu three years earlier. Jordan sucked in a deep breath. *I'm sorry, buddy,* he thought. *This wasn't supposed to happen. But I promise you I'll get the son of a—*

"Everything in order, Dawes?"

Jordan turned rapidly to face Carroll Heumann, the assistant chief of police, now acting chief—and Jordan's boss. Heumann was dressed in a formal blue uniform, though most of the time on the job he wore civilian style suits.

He scowled at Jordan's own dark suit as though it emphasized his being an outsider.

Heumann was a heavy man with more chins than neck and a decided lack of hair. His narrowed brown eyes reflected his no-nonsense outlook. For the moment, they studied Jordan.

Jordan responded to his question. "Far as I can tell,

everything here is as it should be.'' That was a lie, of course. Nothing here was as it should be. Casper Shepard should not be dead. This should not be the day of the funeral of one of the most vital, kind, determined men Jordan had ever met.

''All right,'' Heumann said, joining Jordan beside the doorway to the vestry. The hall where they stood was carpeted with a well-worn, patterned red runner with a blue-and-red border. The walls were textured and dingy white, and dark, dreary paintings of European cathedrals hung here and there. ''There'll be a few cops in town from nearby jurisdictions to keep an eye on things, since most of our people will be attending the funeral. I don't anticipate any trouble, but you never know when it may come, or from where.'' His scrutiny of Jordan's face had intensified.

''No,'' Jordan agreed. ''You don't.'' He wondered if there was a message hidden behind Heumann's words—such as an intimation that trouble came from Texas, just like Jordan.

''Your bride's all right?''

The inquiry seemed belated to Jordan, but he answered willingly. He had every intention of making certain that everyone in the world knew Sara's condition.

It was safer for her that way.

''In most aspects, she seems fine. But that blow to her head—the doctors have no idea if her memory will ever return.''

''She doesn't remember anything now?''

''No,'' Jordan said, looking steadily into his superior's bulldog face. Had he seen a hint of relief flash through his eyes—or was it suspicion? No one was off Jordan's suspect list for now.

He supposed that everyone on the case felt the same way—and that he was at the top of some suspect lists himself. People knew that Casper and he had been arguing.

It had been part of their plan.

"Jordan?" A female voice interrupted his thoughts. It was June Roehmer. She was alone. Jordan felt his features freeze in the fury before the storm; he had told her that she could not leave Sara alone for a moment. She obviously knew what he was thinking, for she said hastily, "Don't worry. Honest. Sara's fine. She's out in the car. Ramon is keeping an eye on her." She hesitated. "I told her about Stu. She didn't remember him, but people here will talk about him today."

"You're right," Jordan acknowledged. "I was going to tell her before things got started, but I'm glad you beat me to it."

After all Sara had been through, he had wanted to protect her from this as long as possible, then break it to her in a manner least calculated to deliver another blow. No good way of presentation had come to him, and he had probably waited too long.

The problem had now been taken from him.

"How did she handle it?"

June shrugged. "Bravely, the way she has dealt with all of this. Is it all right to bring her in?"

"Yes," Jordan said. "In fact, I'll go get her."

Sara's current sitter, Ramon Susa, was June's patrol partner. He had always seemed a little light in the brains department to Jordan, but heavy in Academy-learned police procedure. He was probably as good as anyone for guarding Sara—at least in public. He had been Stu's friend, but there were rumors that they'd had an argument before Stu was killed. Jordan still considered him as much a suspect in Casper's murder, too, as anyone else.

Outside, dozens of cars were beginning to park along the church's wide circular driveway. Many were police patrol cars from Santa Gregoria and other towns all over central California. Their occupants, most in uniform, spilled onto the pavement.

Jordan spotted Ramon, a clean-cut young Latino in uniform, standing near one of the black-and-white police cars. He was leaning down toward the passenger window, apparently conversing with the occupant.

"Hello, Ramon," Jordan said as he reached them. "Thanks for watching Sara for me." He opened the car door. Strain shadowed his new wife's eyes, and her pale complexion contrasted vividly with the black, slightly wavy hair that hung loose to just below her shoulders. She let him help her from the car. "Come inside, Sara." He kept his voice gentle. She didn't say a word as she stood, but shot him a half smile that somehow looked devastated. "June told me you know about Stu now," he told her. "I was going to tell you here, but..." He allowed his voice to trail off.

She nodded slowly. "I suppose everyone else here knows, so it's a good thing I do now, too." She hesitated. "And my mother?" she asked.

"She's gone, too, Sara," Jordan said gently. "She died in an accident when Stu and you were kids."

"I see." There was no measuring the depth of the pain in her voice, so Jordan didn't try.

He couldn't help glancing at the spot where the bandage still lay beneath her hair. How badly did her head still hurt? He kept his arm tightly around her slender shoulders, steering her through the growing crowd. She felt slight against him, but he was still aware—much too aware—of her feminine contours beneath her fitted jacket and flowing suit skirt. When she stumbled once, he kept her from falling.

She glanced up at him and he wanted to erase the gratitude he saw there. It was his fault that she was about to bury her father. "We're nearly there," he growled. He made himself ignore the bewildered tilt of her head at his unkind tone.

The first person to approach as they stepped inside the church was Carroll Heumann. Of course. "I'm sorry for your loss, Sara," he said, his voice gruffer than usual. Maybe he meant it, Jordan thought. "And that you can't remember who did it," he added.

She winced, and Jordan wanted to slug the man. "Me, too," she said softly. "But the doctors assured me that my memory will come back."

"Someday," Jordan interposed as several others on the Santa Gregoria police force joined their small group. "It might take years before she can remember most things. If trauma caused her amnesia, she may never fully recall the event that led to it."

He still held her shoulders, and he could feel her stiffen. "But I—"

He would have interrupted her protestations with a stronger comment, except that June did it for him. "It's all right, Sara," she said. "We're all working on it. You just take care of yourself and let us catch that miserable insect of a serial killer who's done this to your family."

"Serial killer?" Sara looked up at Jordan with surprise. "I didn't realize... Then he—or she—has done this to others, too?"

He nodded. "We'll talk about it later. Right now,

it's time to go sit down in the chapel." He darted a glance at June, who took Sara's hand.

"We'll be with you, Sara," she said. "Won't we, Ramon?"

Her partner nodded. "All of us are behind you, Sara."

People spoke in low tones as they took seats on long wooden pews facing the pulpit. The closed casket had been moved there. It now lay on a pedestal surrounded by flowers whose fragrance flooded the front of the room.

Jordan walked with Sara as June and Ramon preceded them up the aisle to the front row, where they arranged themselves to Sara's left. Jordan didn't sit, not at first. He scowled as he noticed a couple of reporters he'd run into before in the five months since he had been in Santa Gregoria: an anchorwoman from the Channel 8 news, along with her cameraman, and a reporter with the *Santa Gregoria Intelligencer.* Though he knew it wasn't reasonable, he wanted to rush over to them and bodily toss them out. This wasn't a news spectacle; it was a dignified memorial to a man who had deserved to live much longer. The hordes of media, local and national, had been instructed to stay outside. But he would only make the situation worse if he confronted them.

Instead, he sat beside Sara. He took her small hand. It was icy-cold and trembling.

"We'll get through this, Sara," he said, looking straight into her moist hazel eyes. "I promise."

But then he recalled another promise he had made to her—was it only four days earlier? He had promised to love and honor her, to cherish her as his wife.

His promises weren't worth a damn, he thought.

Chapter Three

Jordan's sweet attentiveness was nearly Sara's undoing. As she sat beside him in the pew, she ducked her head, unwilling to allow everyone to see her tears.

"Hold on, Sara," whispered his voice into her ear. Its deep vibration sent shivers of awareness through her. Jordan was here for her. He was her husband. He must love her very much.

And she despised herself for not remembering the deep love she must have for him to have married him. For now, she felt mostly gratitude toward him and a cognizance of his sensuality that had no business here and now.

"I'm fine, Jordan," she told him, and made her crying stop. She smiled at him stoically, pretending not to see the sympathy in his dark blue eyes.

She wept more, though, when the pastor began the service. But much of her sorrow was not because she missed her father. Instead, it was because she missed whatever memories of him she should have.

A lot of people rose one at a time to face the packed church and give testimonials about Casper Shepard. Sara recognized only a few—those who had visited her in the hospital or who had introduced themselves here:

Carroll Heumann, for one. She'd considered the man abrupt with her, but he had apparently thought highly of her father. She believed it when he said he would miss Casper.

Lloyd Pederzani was another person Sara recognized. About fifty, with a gaunt face but kind brown eyes, he had come to her hospital room the evening of her admission. He'd introduced himself as the town's medical examiner, a practicing physician, and a very long-time family friend. He'd looked at her chart, asked how she was feeling and both shaken his head and commiserated about her loss of memory. Then, he had attempted—though poorly—to cheer her up with bad jokes.

Now, Lloyd, in a dark brown suit that bagged at his shoulders, was somber as he described how long Casper and he had been friends. How much he was going to miss the guy who'd called him out of bed at all hours of the night to discuss a new case—though that was certainly one aspect of their friendship he wouldn't miss. His comment drew a laugh from the crowd.

Jordan rose, too, to speak about her father. Her husband remembered the man who had raised her brother and her after their mother had died in an accident years ago.

Sara didn't. That only made her feel worse.

Even the mayor of Santa Gregoria, Pauline Casey, gave the eulogy. Mayor Casey was a slender, older woman with hair the shade of iron—which matched the fist with which she appeared to rule Santa Gregoria, the way she described it. But she spoke fondly of Casper Shepard and how he had given his all to try to make their community safe. She did, however, note that he had not been successful and vowed that whoever succeeded him as police chief would have to make a strong effort to see that no one ever got away with murder here again.

A noble goal, Sara thought. One she hoped would be met. But she shared a dubious glance with Jordan. He winked at her encouragingly, and she attempted a smile.

Sara was glad when the service was over, but then it was time to follow Jordan, Carroll, Lloyd and the other pallbearers outside.

She asked June about the older pallbearer who seemed unashamed of the tears rolling down his grizzled cheeks. He was wrinkled and gray-haired, and wore an unfamiliar uniform that was too small at his rounded middle.

"That's Dwayne Gould," June whispered. "He's a driver for the medical examiner's office. Your father was always kind to him."

Though grateful for June's supportive presence beside her, and Jordan's when he rejoined her, Sara managed just fine, even surviving the lowering of the casket into the newly dug grave.

Afterward, she stood at the graveside beside Jordan, accepting condolences from unfamiliar mourners who apparently knew her well. Jordan introduced many people, apologizing over and over on her behalf. It was not her fault she didn't recognize even those she had known for years, he said; it was a result of her amnesia.

She wanted to strangle the tall, smooth-talking man beside her. During a lull in the surging line of mourners, Sara turned to Jordan. "Please don't keep telling people about my loss of memory," she whispered. "I feel bad enough about it, and if anyone should apologize about it, I should."

"We discussed this before, Sara," he hissed as the line began to move again. "You'll be safer if everyone knows you can't remember anything. And I intend to keep reminding them so it's sure to get to the ears of the killer." And once more, when he introduced her to someone she probably should have recognized, he made reference to her amnesia.

This time, she just gritted her teeth and smiled. She knew he was just trying to protect her.

Why didn't that make her feel any better?

WAS SARA'S AMNESIA REAL?

The Executioner watched Jordan Dawes touch his new wife in public, making a display of his feelings for her.

The Executioner listened, too, for any indication that Sara's loss of memory was a lie.

Of course The Executioner realized that Dawes was trying to protect his pretty wife. The hot-shot Texas Ranger who had so recently come here to Santa Gregoria might have convinced Sara to feign amnesia.

If it were a ploy, it wouldn't work. The Executioner would make an example of Sara and Dawes, then go ahead with other assassinations.

But to continue, The Executioner had to again do whatever was necessary to prevent being caught.

The Executioner had thought it a master stroke to kill Casper Shepard at his own daughter's wedding. But then, each of the assassinations was sublime.

Too bad Sara had followed Casper unexpectedly into the room. Now The Executioner had unfinished business with Sara. Business that needed immediate resolution.

Oh, if Sara truly recalled nothing, perhaps The Executioner would allow her to live. The Executioner had already spoken with her, and she had professed her lack of memory without the slightest hesitation.

But if she really did remember...

Then Sara Dawes would be The Executioner's next piece of superb work.

THE CROWD was beginning to thin. Clouds had started to roll in, chilling the air a little and casting an even more depressing pall on the day. Sara turned on the paved path—and noticed, for the first time, the granite markers on the graves beside the newly dug one for her father.

The nearest read, "Eleanor Markham Shepard, Beloved Wife and Mother," and gave dates of birth and death. *Her* mother? Sara couldn't be certain...but she thought so.

Beside it was another marker that was shorter and not as weathered: Stuart Markham Shepard. Stu. Her brother.

He had been only thirty-three when he had died three years earlier.

How old was *she* now? She wanted to break something, scream out loud, for she didn't remember even something as simple and personal as that. She took a deep calming breath. She would ask Jordan. He would know. And she was certain that Stu had been her older brother.

She stared at his grave...and closed her eyes as a vision of another funeral shimmered before her. She was sobbing. Her father was there. Jordan was there.

And Stu...Stu had been murdered. The Santa Gregoria police force was there en masse, too. She had a sense of being stifled. Of wanting to stab someone, as

Stu had been stabbed. Of wanting to circumvent laws, and law enforcement, which had been so important to all their lives, to avenge him, no matter how—

And then it was gone.

"Sara, are you all right?" It was Jordan. His arms were suddenly around her again, holding her upright. She realized she was swaying. Her mind swirled dizzily and she knew that, without Jordan's strength supporting her, she would have fallen to the ground.

She leaned into him, appreciating his powerful presence. "I—I'm fine," she lied. She moved even closer, pulling his head down so she could whisper into his ear, "Jordan, I just remembered—"

"I'm sorry you're not feeling well, darling," he interrupted. His words were slow and insistent, as though he were speaking to a developmentally challenged child.

She stiffened, then realized he might just be protecting her...again. She glanced around. Though quite a few people still milled around the cemetery, no one was close enough to hear what she said. Why didn't Jordan let her speak?

"Jordan," she began again, "I think my memory might—"

Once more he didn't let her finish. "We'll talk later," he whispered. Out loud, he said, "There's a little reception in memory of your father now, right inside the church. We won't stay long. You need some rest." He started to move her along the paved path, toward a few groups of people and away from the graves.

She let him, though she now wanted to shout at Jordan, too. She appreciated that he was trying to keep her safe. But there was such a thing as being overprotective.

The churchyard was old, full of overhanging trees and large family grave markers. Under other circumstances, Sara would have found it charming.

Now, though, its quaintness only added to her depression. Her family was buried here. Everyone—except for Jordan and her.

And someone had tried to kill her.

Inside a hall within the church, carafes of coffee had been set on tables laden with sliced fruit, donuts and cookies that looked homemade. "I'll get you something to eat," Jordan told her.

"Thanks, but I'm not hungry." In fact, the thought of trying to get any of that sugar down made her stomach roll.

But Jordan caressed her face gently with the side of his hand. The gesture touched her. "You need to keep up your strength, Sara." He took her over to where June and Ramon stood. "Sara's feeling a little peaked," he said. "Keep an eye on her, will you, while I gather some refreshments?"

"Is all of this getting to you?" June's tone was sympathetic. "I'm so sorry, but it's no wonder, with everything that's happened." She looked less pixieish when her eyes reflected sorrow.

"You're a brave lady," Ramon said. His expression was admiring. "Tell me what I can do to help, all right?"

But Sara had nothing to say. There were several things she could think of that would help her, but none that Ramon, kind as his offer was, could hand to her.

The first was her memory. The second was the capture of her father's killer. Her brother's, too. They were probably one and the same.

She glanced at Jordan. Holding a foam plate half filled with food, he was conversing with a couple of uniform cops she didn't recognize.

She turned toward June and Ramon, and found them engrossed in a conversation with one another. They spoke in hushed whispers. June gazed at Sara, then looked guiltily away.

They were talking about *her*. Didn't they think she was bearing up sufficiently under all the strain? Or did they believe she had made up the amnesia?

She didn't care. Even though she had experienced one small but significant snatch of memory in the last few minutes, she really couldn't remember much. And she didn't particularly like the way she was handling the stress, either.

Right now she felt as if the entire funeral, all the guests, were closing in on her. Creating a clutching anxiety deep inside that she needed to flee.

She surreptitiously glanced again toward her temporary keepers, June and Ramon. Neither was looking at her. Jordan, too, still had his attention focused elsewhere.

Sara took the opportunity to slip out of the church.

It was still light outside. There were plenty of people around. Sara needed to be alone.

She wasn't stupid, though. Someone had killed her father and had attacked her. She needed to stay in a crowded place where no one would dare accost her. She didn't go far from the church, choosing to stand in an area that appeared to be one of the cemetery's oldest—judging by how weathered the tall stone markers that nearly surrounded her appeared. The main driveway to the church was behind her; several people were still milling around the parked cars, including media types with cameras, and uniformed cops.

She stood for several minutes enjoying the solitude, despite her sense of incompleteness. She racked her brain, trying to remember more about Stu's funeral—the first significant memory she'd had.

Why had he been killed?

After a while, she felt a few raindrops. She looked up at the darkening sky and sighed. Coming outside had not been such a great idea, after all. She could go back in, find Jordan and ask him to take her home.

She took a few steps toward the church—but someone grabbed her. Something was shoved into her mouth, and she was wrestled sideways and to the ground, facedown, her arms beneath her.

She tried to scream for help, but the gag prevented her from doing more than make a frightened, incoherent noise. What was wrong with all those police? Hadn't anyone seen what happened?

Jordan. Where was he? He'd wanted to protect her. He would save her.

Her assailant kept a knee in the small of her back, pinning her down. He—she?—was strong. Or was it that Sara, scared and still recuperating from her last attack, was weak?

Would she be killed this time?

The right side of her face pressed into earth that was still hard, for the rain was hardly a drizzle. Sara swallowed a whimper. She wouldn't give her attacker the satisfaction of seeing how scared she was.

Where was Jordan?

"Now, Sara Shepard," said a voice that was low and raspy and clearly disguised, "you will answer my very simple questions with a nod or a shake of your head. If you do well, I will let you go and you will be fine. If not, you will be executed prematurely, like your father.''

Sara felt herself stiffen but tried to stay absolutely still—except that she could not prevent her breaths from coming too fast. Something...something niggled at the back of her mind. She had been in this position before. Why? It hadn't frightened her—then.

''Do you understand?'' asked the voice. She heard a few drops of rain softly strike the person's clothing. ''Nod or shake your head.''

Sara made herself give an abrupt nod. She suddenly felt terribly alone. Jordan wasn't coming. He would save her if he knew, but he was inside the church, talking and eating and laughing. He would feel awful when he found her body. But she was on her own.

''Good. Now, tell me—did you see who killed your father?''

That was a question she couldn't actually answer with a yes or no. She didn't know. But what she was certain of was that she didn't remember.

She took the safest course and shook her head in the negative.

''You're lying, Sara Shepard.'' The knee in her back dug in harder, making her gasp in pain. Through her agony, she thought she heard a small sound, like keys jingling—or was it merely the unfamiliar rasp of her own terrified breathing?

Something else teased at the corners of her mind, then disappeared.

''Or should I say Sara Shepard Dawes?'' the voice asked with a sarcastic laugh.

She nodded vehemently to that, although it probably

was not a question her attacker expected her to answer. But the thought once more of Jordan in the church gave her sudden courage. He would have noticed her absence by now and come looking for her.

Wouldn't he?

The voice stormed, "Have you really lost your memory?"

Again she nodded with no hesitation, for it was the truth.

That knee in her back. This position on the ground—

She had taken self-defense courses! Of course she had. Even as a police dispatcher, she had been required to learn the rudiments.

The response came back to her now. Whether it was what she had been taught, or her own take on it, she didn't really know.

"Are you lying, Sara?"

She shook her head carefully, as if too abrupt a movement now would cause her to forget the little bit she had, with so much difficulty, brought back to mind.

She moaned, made her body tremble, and then went limp.

"Sara?" The voice remained disguised, though it sounded a little alarmed.

She didn't move. She just waited, listening to the increasingly heavy rain, listening to her attacker's raspy breathing. Her clothes were damp enough now to stick to her, but she could do nothing about it.

Her assailant remained on her back, though the pressure eased a little. "Sara?" The tone went up a little more.

And then she made her move. Quickly she arched her back, then rolled. It worked! She heard the thud on the dampened earth as the person fell off her.

She pulled herself up into a crouch, prepared to do hand-to-hand combat if necessary. But it wasn't. All she saw of the person was the back of a long, black raincoat, hood raised, as it disappeared behind a tall gravestone.

Chapter Four

Jordan, glad for his rubber-soled dress shoes, loped through the dismal, damp churchyard. His gaze darted everywhere as he assessed the parklike, tree-shrouded area—and searched for Sara. He appeared to be alone out here; everyone else had been smart enough to come in out of the rain.

His fists clenched and unclenched at his sides as his mind listed those he wanted to strangle right then, in ascending order of priority: June Roehmer, Ramon Susa—and Sara.

June and Ramon were cops. Though he wasn't their immediate superior, he had given them an order. Whether or not he could enforce it was irrelevant. They had agreed to keep an eye on Sara. He'd lost track of both of them during the reception, as well as Sara.

The pastor had said he'd seen her leave the church by herself. Where the hell was she?

By now, he was fairly certain that Sara's memory was actually missing, that she wasn't just putting on an act to protect herself. But why hadn't she stayed at the reception, where there were plenty of people around? Perhaps amnesia automatically resulted in a decrease in judgment, too.

He reached the nearest gate to the graveyard—and saw a figure in a long, black raincoat, raised hood over its head, dash from the cemetery into the rear of the churchyard.

Someone just trying to quickly get out of the rain? Maybe. But Jordan's instincts told him otherwise. He closed the gate and ran down the path toward where he had last seen the other person.

But when he got to the rear of the quaint stone church, whoever it was had disappeared. Had he—or she—gone inside?

Jordan wanted to find out, but he still hadn't located Sara, and that was the most important thing. He had no way of knowing whether that person's dash through the rain had anything to do with his wife.

His wife? Why was he thinking of her that way? They were married in name only. That was the plan. Casper's death hadn't changed it.

Still, despite the reasons they had married, she was his to protect.

And she was missing.

He hadn't kept her father from being killed, but he would protect Sara at all costs.

So where was she?

Swallowing his frustration, he went through the rear gate to the cemetery. "Sara?" he called. "Are you out here?" If she were, the logical place for her to be was at the graveside of her family. He went down the path in that direction.

"Jordan?" He had hardly heard his name before she hurtled herself from behind a tall grave marker into his arms, knocking him slightly off balance. He caught himself—and her.

"Sara? Where the devil have you—"

"Did you see the person who attacked me?"

That stopped him from venting his anger. "Attacked you?" He grabbed her shoulders and stepped back, looking down into her face. She was out of breath, and she clung to him. There was a wildness in her hazel eyes that spoke of fear. Her dark hair was plastered in damp tendrils to her head and her smooth, flushed cheeks.

She had never looked more beautiful—and Jordan wanted to kick himself for even noticing such a thing when she was so obviously scared.

"Are you hurt?" he demanded. "Tell me what happened."

He could see how much of an effort the small smile she attempted was. "Could we get out of the rain first?"

"Of course," he rumbled. He put his arm around her shoulders. Her clothes were damp. He removed his own jacket, which was only slightly more dry, and put it around her. Then he led her back into the church.

THE NEXT HOUR was a jumble to Sara. More than once, she wanted to sink to her knees and sob. Mostly, though, she wanted to shout at everyone who asked her questions. Thanks to her ordeal outside and the way her assailant had badgered her, she'd had enough of answering questions to last the rest of her life.

But she knew the people here all wanted to help. To find who had attacked her—for that way, they would also have her father's killer.

Most of the time, Jordan kept an arm protectively around her as they sat in the pastor's private office. It was large but cluttered, with a plain, scratched desk that appeared more well-used than antique. The sofa, though, was new and comfortable, and had a matching love seat.

Sara sat on the sofa beside Jordan.

"Tell us again exactly what happened," Jordan said. He managed to keep from yelling at her, but she saw how much of a strain it was.

Acting Chief of Police, Carroll Heumann, sat on the love seat, which seemed an incongruous location for the large, gruff man. "Why were you outside in the first place?" He made no effort to coddle her. Sara knew he was just doing his job, but she wanted to kick him in the shins and flee from the room.

She sat still, though, and willed herself to maintain her patience.

Also present were June, who sat on a small wooden child's chair she must have found in a Sunday school classroom, and Ramon, who, with arms folded, leaned against the far window. June was uncharacteristically quiet.

In a shaky voice Sara said, "I needed to get away from the crowd." She didn't pause to wait for the criticisms and recriminations she knew everyone was thinking, but continued, "I thought I was being careful. There were plenty of people outside. But it started to rain, and whoever it was just grabbed me and dragged me behind a tall gravestone."

She felt Jordan's substantial body shift slightly, as though her very words made him fume. She swallowed a sigh of misery. She didn't blame him; in hindsight, she realized that, though she had thought she had done what she needed to keep her sanity, it had been foolish.

But now she needed his support and understanding. And she could not be certain he would give it.

"How tall was he?" Jordan asked. At least his voice was calm.

She tried to make her shrug seem nonchalant. She didn't want him to know how she ached inside. "Taller than me, I think. But that impression could just have been because he—or she—took me unawares and overpowered me so easily."

"Did you hear or see anything that would allow you to recognize the person again?"

Something nudged the edges of Sara's mind. Had there been something identifiable? Maybe...but her sorry excuse for a brain wasn't latching onto it right then.

Any more than it was giving her the rest of the answers she needed.

This time she did sigh out loud. "No."

"Go ahead, then," Jordan said in a kind tone. "Tell us what you do remember."

Sara noticed the scowl Heumann shot Jordan. Was it because he thought he should be asking the questions?

Hurriedly, so as not to foment more animosity between the two men, Sara described her latest ordeal. When she was finished, she said, "I know that doesn't give you a lot to go on to catch the suspect. The voice was disguised, so I couldn't even tell for sure if it was male or female. The person was definitely strong, though. I couldn't turn around to see his identity. And...and he—or she—didn't believe I'd lost my memory, at least not initially." She didn't mention that a smattering of it had come back during the crisis; she wanted to mull that over herself first. Perhaps even discuss it with Jordan. Shouldn't her husband know that her amnesia might not be complete or permanent?

Might it already be obvious? She didn't recall how it felt to be a police dispatcher, but she was easily slipping back into using law enforcement terminology.

"I'm sorry I can't tell you more," she finished.

"So am I," Carroll Heumann said. "You shouldn't have gone out alone like that, but since you did, it would have been a perfect opportunity to nab the perpetrator."

"She could have been hurt," reminded June Roehmer, her critical words to her superior tempered by a sympathetic smile toward Sara.

"Again," added Ramon, without budging from his position near the window.

Sara noted that Jordan added nothing to that part of the conversation. Shouldn't her husband express further concern for her safety?

He had come looking for her. He had found her. He had treated her tenderly while taking her inside, just as he had after the attack that had killed her father.

But she yearned for something more from him—a greater show of affection. Something that would make it clearer to her why they had married. That they loved each other.

"One thing, just for clarification," Jordan said. "We should each describe where we were while Sara was being attacked."

Heumann appeared almost apoplectic. "You surely don't think that I—"

"I don't think anything," Jordan said mildly. "I just want to rule out as many suspects as possible. I was on my cell phone in an alcove. I doubt anyone saw me there, so I haven't an alibi. No one appears wet from the rain—though the person I saw wore a hooded coat. Where were you, June?"

She had been in the ladies' room—alone. Ramon had gone out behind the church, under an overhang, for a cigarette. Reluctantly, Heumann told them that he had been in one of the church's Sunday school classrooms checking it out for his grandkids.

Sara realized that none of them could be ruled out as a suspect. But surely her assailant couldn't have been one of them—could it?

Beside her, Jordan stood. "Sara, you stay here with June for a while. I have something I need to do."

There was a grim determination on his masculine face. She wouldn't have wanted to cross him then.

But what was he going to do? Make sure he hadn't left any clues that would identify him as her attacker?

That was a nasty shot, Sara castigated herself. Even if there was something a little off in the way Jordan, her new husband, treated her, she had no reason to think him a suspect in her father's death or in the attacks on her.

Except that June had told her that Jordan and her father had been arguing....

No, whatever Jordan was up to, she could be certain it would be in her best interests.

She lifted her face up to him for a kiss. Wasn't that what new brides did?

He blinked in what appeared to be surprise and uncertainty before he caught himself and bent toward her. His lips were cool, and their contact with hers brief. Unsatisfying.

"See you later," he said over his shoulder as he strode out of the room.

Bewildered and hurt, Sara nevertheless noticed the expressions on the faces of the others as they stared after Jordan. Ramon's mouth quirked slightly in an amused smile that did not erase the uneasiness in his eyes.

June appeared perturbed, but her eyes seemed glued to Jordan's compact butt, hugged by his dress trousers. A pang of something that could have been jealousy caromed through Sara. That was her husband's behind that June so obviously admired.

But there was nothing at all appreciative of Jordan Dawes in Carroll Heumann's snide grimace.

"I'M SORRY I left you with that cheery crowd," Jordan said to Sara a while later. He shot an ironic glance toward her from the driver's seat of his white Mustang. The arch expression went wonderfully with Jordan's masculine features, turning them roguish and utterly appealing.

No wonder Sara had fallen in love with him…hadn't she?

She was beginning to believe so, more and more. But if she could now remember a little of her police training, why couldn't she recall how she felt about her brand-new husband?

Jordan continued, "I knew Heumann had ordered an investigation of what happened to you, but I wanted to start one of my own."

"Did you learn anything?" Sara asked.

"Only that our perpetrator is pretty damned cunning. I believe I spoke with everyone at the funeral, though briefly. Most had milled around, talking to one another, speculating on who killed your father. Though only one person planned it that way, they generally provided great alibis for one another. No one paid a lot of attention as to those who might have wandered off by themselves."

Sara felt shocked. "You're really pushing it, aren't you? You weren't just trying to rule out suspects before. You really think that one of my father's friends attacked me—someone on the Santa Gregoria force?"

Jordan's tone was gentle as he answered, though he did not move his eyes from the road in front of them. "Yes, Sara, I do."

"But—"

"We'll talk about it one day when you're stronger. For now, take a look in front of us. Does this street seem familiar?"

She peered through the windshield toward a wide avenue lined on both sides with pleasant-looking stucco houses, most with at least some expanse of green lawn. There were eucalyptus trees and a few oaks, and cars of fairly current vintages sat by the curbs or in driveways. It seemed a pretty neighborhood, welcoming, a nice enough place to live. But did anything look familiar? She strained her memory and came up with...nothing.

"Not really. Is it supposed to?"

Jordan nodded, then pulled the car to the curb and looked toward her. A thatch of his light brown hair had slipped from where he had brushed it back from his face to curl winsomely over his broad forehead. He had deposited his jacket and tie onto the back seat, and his white shirt was open at the neck, revealing a hint of chest hair a few shades darker than that on his head. "Don't worry about it. You'll remember everything, one of these days."

It would have been a perfect opportunity to tell Jordan about how she had fought off her attacker earlier—how her training had come back to her.

But she didn't tell him. Not yet.

Though her mind had helped her in a crisis, the knowledge of a few self-defense techniques seemed like such a minor matter, compared with how she felt about the man beside her.

She wanted to be able to fling herself into his arms and tell him she remembered how they had met. How they had fallen in love. What their wedding had been like.

Until those memories had returned, nothing else was important.

He had come around to the passenger side of the car and opened the door. He helped her out.

She glanced toward the house before them. It was a pretty dwelling, a two-story gray stucco with white trim at the doors and windows, small white wrought-iron balconies outside the two upstairs windows, and a riot of flowers in beds on either side of the walkway to the front porch.

A tiny pang of recollection seemed to jolt Sara. "It *does* look familiar!" she exclaimed. She turned excitedly toward Jordan, unconsciously holding out her hands. He took them as she said, "Jordan, tell me about the house. Did we pick it out together before we got married?"

The pleased expression seemed to vanish from his face, and his deep blue eyes grew fathomless once more. "No, Sara." His voice was soft, as though he were talking with a child. Didn't he understand that only made her feel worse? "It's your house. You lived here with your father. Stu grew up here, too. Now it'll belong to you."

To *her*. Not to *them?* Something inside Sara seemed to shrivel into a choking tightness. Maybe technically she would be the one to inherit the place—did she even want it? But Jordan and she would live here together.

Or—

Not looking at him, not wanting to see the expression on his face when she asked her next question, or when he answered, she began to walk up the paved path toward the house. The flowers she had seen from the car enveloped her in their luscious fragrance, and she inhaled deeply. Then she said, "Where did we plan to live after we got married, Jordan?"

She stopped walking so she could hear his reply. She felt his presence close by her, though he didn't touch her. "Right here." His deep voice rumbled from above and just behind her right ear.

"With my father?" She continued up the path. Why didn't any of this feel right? Hadn't she wanted privacy to be with her beloved new husband?

Or had she cared so deeply for her father that she hadn't wanted to leave him alone, even after she was married?

And Jordan had agreed to that? He must also have thought a lot of her father. Casper Shepard must have been a wonderful man—and she couldn't remember him.

She'd had the opportunity twice now to learn the identity of his murderer—and had failed to do so. She had failed her father.

What was the matter with her? Surely not all people who were struck on the head lost their memories. Why had she?

Jordan interrupted her self-castigation by answering her question. "Yes, we decided to stay with Casper for a while." He moved around her and unlocked the white front door. He pushed it open for her. "Welcome home, Sara."

She took a step toward the entry...then halted. She turned to face Jordan, who remained at her side. She knew her glance must have been quizzical, and his brows furrowed in a responsive question of his own.

He didn't get it. Maybe this man she married wasn't a romantic. Maybe that hadn't mattered to her, when she'd had her memory.

But wasn't a new groom supposed to carry his bride over the threshold?

It didn't matter. Not in the greater scheme of things. She took another step forward—and suddenly she was swept up into his arms.

He carried her as though she weighed no more than the clothes she wore. He held her against his strong chest, and she threw her arms around his neck. She laughed, half in relief and half in the joy of being close to him. Oh, yes, even if she couldn't recall it, she must love this man. She planted a happy kiss at the side of his mouth.

Once they were inside the entryway, he gently put her down. "Welcome, Sara," he repeated. "That's what you wanted, wasn't it? To be carried over the threshold?"

She felt as though a pin had been thrust into her flesh, bursting the balloon that had been her momentary happiness. Yes, she had wanted it. But more than that, she had wanted *him* to want it.

She needed to know more about their relationship. Right now. She simply couldn't wait until the ephemeral attribute that was her memory returned.

"Jordan, could I talk with you for a few minutes?"

A leeriness passed across his handsome face, turning

it blank and a little fearsome. But she wouldn't be intimidated. She couldn't allow it. She waited for his answer.

"Of course," he finally said. "I'll go make us some cappuccino in the kitchen, then we can sit at the table and talk."

That sounded heavenly! And…it sounded familiar. As though it was something they had done before! "Jordan, have we ever had cappuccino in the kitchen together?"

He nodded, a smile partially eradicating the worrisome expression on his face. "The three of us—your father, you and I. We spent hours together talking over…talking in the kitchen. The cappuccino-maker was Casper's. He loved playing with it, and his concoctions were usually great."

A feeling of warmth rushed over Sara. Her father. In the kitchen, over cappuccino…with Jordan. Did she recall it?

Jordan echoed, "Did you remember, Sara?"

"I—I'm not sure." But she could feel the wide smile on her face. "I think maybe I do. Let's go in and find out, shall we?"

She put out her hand—then froze. Would he take it? Somehow, though she wasn't sure why, she wondered.

But in a moment her hand was held in Jordan's firm grasp. Together, they walked down the hall and into the kitchen. Sara led the way.

But was it memory or instinct that guided her steps?

"THIS CAPPUCCINO is great!" Sara said a while later, facing her husband across the worn butcher-block table.

The kitchen hadn't looked familiar, though it appeared a cozy place where a family could gather. There was a cooking island in the middle, complete with a work area surfaced in bright Mexican tile and a metal grill that was dingy and scratched enough to proclaim a lot of use over many years. The cabinets were pale pine, and the refrigerator yellow and huge, containing a water dispenser and ice-maker in the door.

It was a charming, welcoming room, with a faint aroma of baking cinnamon rolls hovering in the air. But it struck no memories in Sara.

Neither had the upstairs. Before making their drinks, Jordan had taken her there, shown her that her bedroom was the second door on the left. Her father's master suite was just down the hall, and Stu's childhood room had been the one just across from hers. Stu had lived in an apartment, though, at the time of his death, Jordan had told her.

Her room was decorated in shades of burgundy and blue. Had she always lived here, or had she ever taken an apartment, too? She couldn't remember.

Hers was a pretty room, but she'd seen no indication that Jordan had moved any of his clothing into it. He had probably been waiting for her to come home.

Now, Jordan sat across from her, leaning back on a stiff wooden chair that, like hers, had a puffy orange-print pillow tied onto the seat.

It was time for Sara to learn the answers to some questions. Taking a deep breath, she asked, "Tell me how we met."

Jordan's foaming cup of cappuccino sat on the table in front of him, half drunk. He stared into it for a moment, as though pondering whether to answer, then began. "I knew your brother Stu before I met you. He and I both joined the Navy SEALs about fourteen years ago. We became good friends and sometimes spent our leaves visiting each other's families.''

Fourteen years earlier. That would have made Sara sixteen, and Stu twenty-two…. When she'd asked, Jordan had told her she had just turned thirty. Stu's gravestone had allowed her to do the arithmetic; her brother had been six years older than she.

''Did I meet you when you came home with Stu?'' she asked.

Jordan nodded, his large hand reaching for his cup. He had rolled up the sleeves of his white shirt, exposing his sinewy forearms. He took a sip, placing his full upper lip over the rim of the cup and closing his eyes briefly, as though in enjoyment.

Sara felt a stirring warmth ooze through her, deep inside. She doubted he had meant the action to be the slightest bit sexy…but it was. *Jordan* was.

And here she was, home alone for the first time after their wedding, with her brand-new husband. Though she didn't exactly feel married to him, no longer was he a total stranger to her, either. No wonder she was thinking lustful thoughts.

But it was still early in the evening. Right now, she just wanted to get to know him better.

He rose and left the kitchen. When he returned, he held out a framed photograph of three people around a Christmas tree. Sara took it from him. She recognized herself, though she was several years younger. She inhaled deeply as she recognized her father: the whitehaired man who had been lying on the hotel room floor. She couldn't recall the younger, dark-haired man who resembled her, but obviously he was Stu.

She shook her head ruefully. The picture triggered no memories.

"You were already the woman of the family when I met you," Jordan said. He had sat down in his chair. The faraway smile on his face suggested he was indulging in a pleasant bout of nostalgia, and it brought an answering smile to Sara's lips. "I used to love to come here to enjoy all the wonderful meals you prepared for us—Mexican enchiladas, All-American pot roast, German wieners and sauerkraut...with all that international know-how, you certainly got my attention. I had the impression that you did a great job of cooking for your dad, too, but always prepared special meals for Stu and me when we visited."

"I wanted to impress my big brother that much, huh?" Sara glanced again at the photo, then put it down on the table.

"Stu was definitely impressed—but figured it wasn't him you wanted to dazzle. He gave me strict orders not to mess with his little sister, no matter how much of a crush she might have on me."

Sara felt her face redden. "What made you think I had a crush on you?"

"Isn't the old expression, 'The fastest way to a man's heart is through his stomach'? Besides, you seemed to find a lot of excuses to hang out with us, needing to go shopping at the mall when we went, just dying to see whatever movies we intended to go to—"

"I might just have wanted to hang out with the guys. Or maybe I was trying my fledgling female wings and intended that *you* develop a crush on *me* so I could break your heart." She laughed. But Sara suspected Jordan had been right. She had apparently fallen for him fourteen years earlier. No wonder she had been ready to marry him now.

She wished, though, that she could recall all that had

happened to both of them in the interim. It surely hadn't taken her all that time to grow up and mature.

Patience, she told herself. Her memory would return. It had to. At least her head didn't hurt so much now.

And in the meantime, she would continue to ask questions. "How long were Stu and you in the SEALs?"

"Four years."

"Was it tough?" Sara was aware that the special SEALs forces required superior physical training and skills. She bit her lower lip. Why was it that she remembered what to her should be trivial, but recalled so little of major importance?

"It was an exciting time, taught us a lot, but neither of us wanted to make a career of it." As he spoke, he absently stroked the slight shadow of a beard on his cheeks with the backs of his fingers, and Sara wondered how scratchy it felt.

"And afterward?" Sara took a final sip and put the cup she had been holding on the table. "What did you both do? Did you keep in touch?"

"Yes, we stayed in close contact. We still had a lot in common, though Stu came back here and I went home to Dallas." Hence his slight but definite Southern accent, obviously Texan. "We both went into law enforcement. Stu took some training and joined the Santa Gregoria police force with your father."

"Wasn't that nepotism?" Sara asked. Of course, now she knew that she, too, was in local law enforcement. She had a vague recollection that hiring relatives was often frowned on, at least some places.

"I asked Stu about that once. He said that there were few enough people interested in joining the force here that Santa Gregoria had passed an ordinance permitting more than one person in the same family to be hired as long as no one was treated more favorably than anyone else in the same position.''

"I see. And you—what did you do?''

"I became a Texas Highway Patrol Trooper for eight years. Then I joined the Texas Rangers.''

No wonder he remained in such great condition. Or at least Sara believed so, judging by the way his muscles seemed to bulge out the sleeves of his shirt. And she had felt firsthand the steeliness of his hard chest.

Once again, she felt a surge of sexual awareness flood every inch of her. Maybe…maybe bedtime could be a little earlier. They were, after all, newlyweds.

There was a lot more she wanted to learn from him, of course—about her family, and about how her relationship with Jordan had progressed from a teenage crush to full-fledged love.

And how she had finally convinced the man she was no longer an immature kid, but a woman worthy of his love, too.

But they would have plenty of time tomorrow, and the tomorrows after that. Right now, they had other things to learn about each other.

Or had they partaken in such delights before? Sara closed her eyes, feeling a pain wash through her that had nothing to do with physical discomfort. Damn her memory! At least she should be able to remember *that*.

"Sara, are you all right?'' Jordan's deep voice radiated concern. She opened her eyes to find him regarding her with a questioning solemnity that nearly made her want to cry.

"Just a little tired,'' she replied. "I think I'm ready to go to bed. How about you?'' She lowered her head a little and looked up at him through her lashes. She even licked her lips. Was that too blatant?

"Oh, I'm doing fine," he said, standing to clear her cup off the table. He left his own, which still contained some cappuccino. "I have some paperwork to take care of, then there's a show on television I've been wanting to see. I'll head upstairs in an hour or so, don't worry about me."

"Fine." He hadn't gotten the message. Should she be more direct? "Other than being a little tired, I feel really great now. Ready for...anything. If I'm asleep when you come up to bed, please wake me, okay?"

He didn't even turn around from where he stood, rinsing the cup in the sink. "That's not necessary, Sara. You need your rest. I've moved into Stu's room, so I won't disturb you."

"Right," Sara said, hating the way her voice cracked. She didn't want him to know how hurt she felt. What good would it do? "See you tomorrow."

Chapter Five

Clutching the frame to the kitchen door so hard that he was afraid he would crack the wood, Jordan watched as Sara climbed the stairs. Though he was behind her, he could tell by the tilt of her head that her tapered, determined chin was raised proudly. He observed the gentle sway to her hips that moved her flowing brown skirt as she walked. He had noticed that motion before—and it drove him nuts.

Sara drove him nuts. What on earth had ever possessed him to agree to this plan?

"Because I need your help," said a voice in his memory. Casper Shepard's. He had heard it over the phone—had it been only six months ago? "For Stu's sake," the old man had said in a sad but decisive tone. "That's why you should at least come here, talk it over."

He watched as Sara reached the top of the steps. She turned and saw him standing there. Her hand reached uncertainly for the bandage at the side of her head. He couldn't see the expression in her lovely hazel eyes from here but knew they would not contain the need he had glimpsed in them earlier. The need that mirrored his own—but could not be fulfilled.

That they were married did not matter. Sara didn't know the entire story.

Tell her, a voice inside him—his conscience, perhaps, if he had one—demanded. *Explain it to her now.*

But if he did, he couldn't wake her as she'd suggested. Take her into his arms, show her what a wedding night should be—

He ground his teeth. *Not even you are that much of a lowlife,* he told himself.

Was he?

"Good night, Sara," he made himself call cheerfully.

She inclined her head, then turned her back on him again to walk down the hall.

He pivoted and went back into the kitchen. He glanced around for a moment until he realized he was searching for something to slam against the wall.

Instead, he made himself approach the table slowly, then sink back into the seat he had occupied earlier.

The same seat Casper had designated as his the night he had arrived in Santa Gregoria a couple of weeks after Casper's call to discuss this foolhardy scheme.

The scheme that had been designed to catch Stu's killer.

The scheme that had, instead, led to Casper's death. And Sara's injury and amnesia.

"Dammit!" Jordan said through clenched teeth. He vaguely became aware of a pain in his hand and looked down. Without realizing it, he had picked up the cup that had contained his cappuccino and crushed it. Blood oozed from a gash on his palm.

He rose and rinsed the wound at the sink, noticing with detachment that the cut wasn't very deep. Not that he would have run off to the emergency room for stitches even if it were. He had to stay to protect Sara. And right now, he deserved anything he got.

He wrapped a paper towel around his hand to catch any residual bleeding. "Okay, Casper," he whispered into the empty kitchen, "what do I do now?"

Catch the son of a blessed blue witch, came the reply in his mind, as clearly as if Casper had actually been here, speaking it. *Catch the skunk who did this to my family.*

Of course that was what Jordan would do. That was what his years with the Texas Rangers had taught him. That was why he had come.

But in the meantime, what would he do with Sara?

Don't mess with my sister. This time it was Stu's voice intruding into Jordan's mind. Stu had said those words to him plenty of times in the past. Not that he'd had any dishonorable intentions toward Sara then—at least none that he would ever have acted on, for as sweet and sexy and enticing as she'd been, she had still been a kid. One who'd had a crush on him, of course, which had made her all the more appealing—but none the less off-limits.

He'd known from Stu when Sara had married five years earlier. He had thought of her now and then before that, considered whether she had grown up, asked Stu about her in the same breath that he asked about Casper. Nothing overly eager, though he had wondered about her.... But the news of her marriage had dissipated all his little unfulfilled fantasies.

Until Casper had called and suggested his ridiculous plan: Jordan would marry Sara.

She had been divorced by then. While they were hatching their plot, she had assured him she didn't mind the charade, for it was designed to capture the person who had murdered her beloved brother. And after her disaster of a marriage, she'd had no intention of ever being actually wedded again.

Thanks to the evidence Casper had only recently discovered, there had been reasons why they'd had to make it look so real that it *was* real.

While he was considering whether to agree, his fantasies had returned. And if Sara shared them…well, they were two consenting adults.

But Sara's consent right now would be based on a misconception: that they were married in more than name.

Why hadn't he told her before, when he'd had the chance? That would have made that come-hither look in her eyes turn into a message to stay far, far away.

When he had returned to Santa Gregoria to marry her, she had been friendly, though aloof. If he had thought he'd glimpsed appreciation in her eyes…well, clearly it had been his imagination. He'd missed the schoolgirl crush—especially since Sara Shepard had grown from a pretty teenager to a woman who would make the most devotedly celibate man's eyes pop. And that didn't describe Jordan in the least.

Not that he'd wanted attachment, either. He intended to return to his career as a Texas Ranger. Plus, he didn't believe in foolishness like forgiveness or second chances—his or anyone else's. His father, an army sergeant, had long drilled that into Jordan. He had been right.

Jordan wouldn't leave here until he had nabbed the SOB who had killed Stu…and Casper.

Jordan hadn't prevented Casper's murder. He deserved nothing from Sara but contempt.

But Sara had forgotten why he was here and the

rules of their arrangement. She didn't know her father's death was the result of Jordan's failure. To her, their marriage was for the conventional reason. And so, she mistakenly had an interest in him as a man, not just as a skilled, outside investigator....

He couldn't take advantage of her. He would tell her the truth in the morning.

And for now? *Go take a cold shower, Dawes,* he told himself, heading for the stairway.

"GOOD MORNING." Sara attempted to sound cheerful as she puttered around the kitchen, trying to remember what she liked for breakfast. Cereal and milk, wasn't it? And a half grapefruit, when good ones were available.

Odd, the things she remembered. Like cologne. She had found a lemon scent on her dresser and put a little on. It seemed familiar.

And coffee. She'd had no trouble at all finding the ground beans in the freezer and brewing a pot that had come out quite well, she proudly told herself.

Had it been her brother or father who'd taught her how? She glanced at the Christmas photo that she had propped on the kitchen table: herself, with her father, her brother....

They were gone. Even if she remembered everything about them, she would never see them again. Or her mother.

Thank heavens she had Jordan.

"Morning," Jordan finally muttered in response to her greeting. He poured himself some coffee and clunked it down on the table, then sat in the same chair he'd taken last night. He put his hands around his coffee mug, then pulled one away and shook it, as though it hurt.

"What did you do to your hand?" Sara asked.

Jordan only shrugged. He didn't look as though it were a good morning. He had thrown a blue shirt over his shoulders without buttoning it, though the way his broad shoulders were slouched, not much of his chest was visible. His trousers were fastened, though his belt wasn't, and his feet were bare. He hadn't shaved yet, and his eyes were at half mast. He appeared exhausted—and as sexy as anyone Sara could ever remember seeing.

Or sexier than anyone she would remember if she had a memory, she amended in her mind...and smiled.

"What's so funny?" he demanded grumpily.

"Ah, we obviously have a real morning person here. Did I know that before I married you?"

"You didn't know much about me before you married me," he retorted.

"Then I must have been bowled over by your charm later in the day." Sara didn't feel as buoyant as she made herself sound, either. She hadn't slept much—half hoping that she'd misunderstood Jordan. That he would appear in her room sometime in the night and use that stunningly sensual physique of his to rock her to her newlywedded toes.

But he hadn't come to her. She had heard the shower running, though, at least twice.

All she could hope now was that his grouchiness was at least in part due to his own lack of sleep.

But why would he avoid his new bride in bed?

It was better that way, of course, since he was, after all, a stranger. Still...

She intended to ask him, but before she could get

up the nerve, he said, "I'll need to go to the station today to work on a bank robbery case—and to check on how things are progressing on the investigation into your father's murder. You can stay there for a while so I can get some work done. Even if someone on the force is our perpetrator, it's unlikely you'll be bothered there with everyone under orders to keep an eye on you."

"I won't like being watched like that," Sara said, "but otherwise that sounds great. I'll get back to work, too."

"Work?" His deep blue eyes suddenly fully open, he looked at her. "What do you mean?"

She sighed. "Jordan, when I was attacked in the cemetery, a little piece of my memory returned. You'd already told me I was a police dispatcher. I recalled I was employed by the Santa Gregoria police and had taken self-defense training. That was how I fought the creep off—by using techniques I'd learned. I've been thinking about it. I can't figure out the whys and wherefores of my memory loss—I still can't recall people or events. But I remember enough about my job to go back to work."

She only wished she remembered more about her feelings toward Jordan. Lust—yes; she felt it now. Love?

Oh, yes, something inside her shouted. But something else contradicted it. She'd liked the guy, sure. What red-blooded American woman wouldn't?

But love? She sensed, somehow, a brittle glass door shutting her off from love. But how could that be?

Jordan stood and approached her. She had just found the cereal bowls and placed one on the tile counter. He towered over her, and she was certain he wanted her to feel intimidated as he glared.

She wouldn't give him the satisfaction. She stood her ground, tilting her head as she looked up at him with a mocking expression on her face. "Are you trying to tell me something?" she asked.

"You should have mentioned that before, Sara. I need to know when any parts of your memory return— but you have to be careful not to tell anyone else."

"I didn't intend to tell *anyone*." She let her irritation show in her voice.

"I'm on your side," he retorted. "I'm the only one you can be sure of, and—"

"How?" she demanded. She took a step toward him, hands on her hips as she glared up at him. "How can I be certain even *you're* trustworthy? The little bit I remember doesn't tell me anything about you. And though you've been kind and protective, you've hardly been a loving husband—" She stopped, throwing one hand over her mouth. She hadn't intended to say anything to him that might sound like criticism. Or begging. "Never mind." She turned her attention back to her cereal.

"Sara, look." His voice behind her was kind. He put his hands on her shoulders, and she made herself pull away. "There are things you don't know."

She rounded on him. "What a surprise! I realize there's a lot I don't know, Jordan. Maybe you can enlighten me."

He opened his mouth as though he might do just that—but his cell phone rang.

And Sara wanted to scream.

He answered it. "Dawes. That's it? We'll be there in a few." He pressed the button, then looked at Sara apologetically. "The team that was supposed to go over the cemetery with a fine-toothed comb claims that all they found where you were assaulted was one of the memorial sheets they passed out at Casper's funeral a few minutes before that. They've dusted for prints and found nothing. But I want to see it before it's filed away."

Again, he took her shoulders, but this time they were face-to-face. "Sara, there's so much I'm sorry for, so much you need to know...but I don't want to hurry the explanation. We'll talk later, okay?"

What choice did she have? "Okay," she said with a sigh.

"YOU DON'T NEED TO do this." Jordan's voice was a growl, and Sara knew that he intended her to interpret his words as a command to *not* reassume her position as police dispatcher.

"Of course I don't," she agreed sweetly. "But I want to." With that, despite being utterly conscious of Jordan hovering over her shoulder, she turned back to Izzy Wilson, the dispatcher she was about to replace.

Izzy, short for Isabelle, was a pretty, dark-complected woman in the usual navy-blue uniform. She had a quick, quirky smile and a generous attitude as she patiently refreshed Sara in the art of dispatching, as though this were her first day on the job after a long absence.

Which, to all intents and purposes, it was. But to Sara's surprise and delight, dispatching was one of the things that leaped right back into her memory. All she needed was a reminder or two.

"So if I get a 9-1-1 call, I have to interpret whether it's a real emergency or not," Sara repeated back to

Izzy. "In any case, I record it as an incident in the proper computer file." She ran her fingers along the keyboard and came up with the template to start logging a new incident. "If it's an emergency, then I transmit it by computer to the closest of the black-and-white unit that's clear, so they can go investigate, or I forward it to the fire department, with a notation whether their EMTs will be needed. If it's a real priority—a 'hot shot'—I also broadcast it by microphone to make sure it's not overlooked by someone who's not in his unit keeping an eye on the mobile computer terminal."

"You got it, Sara." Izzy sounded as proud as if she had just taught an elementary school pupil how to read. "You can work into it gradually, since you were injured. I'll be around for a couple of hours. I pitched in for some healthy overtime to help while you weren't available, but I've other things to catch up on now. I can help you while I'm here if something comes up that you can't handle." She paused, then said, "Then the next shift starts. Soon as you're up to it, you'll take a full shift on your own. Santa Gregoria's equipment isn't quite state of the art, but we're getting there—and we're too small to have more than one dispatcher on duty most of the time."

Sara nodded. Santa Gregoria, from what she had seen of it since her memory loss, appeared to be a moderate-size town. She didn't recall its population, although she did know it was in Central California. Strange, the things her memory had retained. She wasn't sure how large its police force was, but her screen indicated perhaps ten black-and-whites on patrol just then.

As she looked over the computer, telephone and radio equipment, she swallowed any sense of misgiving.

She had done this before. She even remembered doing it, and, according to Izzy, she had done it quite well. Now, she could do it again.

She ran her eyes down the list of "Ten Code" numbers used for simplified communications by police and dispatchers. The meanings of most came back to her as she reviewed them, not only the easy, familiar ones such as "Ten Four," which meant a message was received, but also such codes as "Ten Fifty-eight," a garbage complaint.

She sat back contentedly in her chair. At least something was going well.

She glanced up at Jordan, who shrugged and shot her an amused smile. He might not be thrilled with her determination, but at least he appeared to be a good sport about it.

"Go ahead with your investigation," she told him. "Leave the dispatching to me." She heard the pride in her voice. For the first time in days she was going to be doing something worthwhile, and on her own.

"At least you'll know how to find me if you need me." He pulled his cell phone from the holster on his belt and waved it at her. She had his number.

In fact, she had made herself memorize it first thing—partly to prove to herself that, at least in this, her mind was functioning.

"I most certainly have your number, Mr. Dawes," she agreed.

"Then I'll see you soon, Mrs. Dawes," he said.

The words jolted Sara. *Mrs. Dawes.* She was Jordan's wife, and no matter how he treated her when they were alone, he was waving a banner about it when they were in public.

For her protection? The idea made her feel pleased

and melty inside—till she thought about the fact that he could hardly keep an eye on her when he was out in the field investigating.

Still, his name enveloped her in a mantle of security, even when he wasn't near. She was in the middle of a police station—a small one, to be sure, shoehorned into the first floor of the same building that housed the offices of the Santa Gregoria mayor and the city council meeting rooms, not to mention the library. But it still was the headquarters of an actual, dynamic law enforcement agency.

And she was the wife of Jordan Dawes, expert police detective and investigator, former Texas Ranger.

No one would hurt her here.

She moved her head slightly to watch her husband as he went from cubicle to cubicle in the tiny police station, making small talk with the uniformed officers who occupied the bullpen of desks—and undoubtedly telling everyone to keep an eye on her, as he'd insisted earlier. As a detective, Jordan wore clothing of his own choice rather than a uniform. Today he had on an off-white shirt with dark amber buttons, a wide belt that he must have worn as a Texas Ranger, and even cowboy boots beneath his khaki trousers. She had seen him strap on a shoulder holster beneath his suede vest. His badge hung from a pocket at his hip. He had a small bandage on his hand but hadn't told her how he'd hurt it.

Watching his sensual, limber form, Sara considered once more how lonely she had been in her bed last night...and sighed.

She herself wore a navy-blue uniform with brass buttons. It was slightly large on her; she had apparently lost weight over the last, difficult days. She assumed that such clothing was the appropriate attire for a dispatcher in Santa Gregoria after finding several uniforms in a place of honor in one end of her bedroom closet that morning. But, more than that, she had wanted to don the uniform. She had remembered that it was right for her. That she always wore a uniform on the job. Her job. Her *life*. At least another small piece of the puzzle that was her memory had returned that morning, jogged by seeing the uniforms.

But as a dispatcher, she wasn't a full-fledged officer. Izzy had told her that. She had found her badge, at least, that identified her as a dispatcher.

She didn't recall how she had worn her hair before to appear professional. She'd finally, just that morning, been able to remove her bandage. Today, she had clipped her black waves up behind her ears, allowing it to hang free down her back. Had she normally pinned it up? Maybe she should have asked Jordan.

She glanced up to see him enter the doorway at the perimeter of the room that led to his tiny office. He reappeared a while later, carrying a notebook and some files, then returned to her side. "I've looked over the cemetery crime scene report. It's time now for me to hit the road. You stay here, Sara, and I'll be back for you in a few hours."

"Fine," she said. She didn't have time to ask about her hair; he was out the door in moments...just as the 9-1-1 phone on her desk rang.

For the next couple of hours, Sara was incredibly busy. Patrol officers forwarded their locations often, and she had to keep track of each of them by computer. Some she sent to check out reports of altercations and other problems phoned in by civilians, most coming in on the 9-1-1 line.

At first, she felt overwhelmed, but then it seemed to meld into a routine. A *familiar* routine. She might not remember each second of her life before, but this definitely felt right.

At one point when Izzy spelled her, Sara walked toward the door to the largest office at the perimeter of the police department—and stopped. What had she been doing?

The sign on the door still read, Casper Shepard, Chief of Police.

Unconsciously, she realized, she had intended to pop her head into her father's office to say hi—as if she had done it a hundred times before. More likely, it had been a thousand.

She glanced around. Had anyone noticed? It didn't seem so, for the bullpen was nearly empty at this hour approaching lunch.

No one should be able to glean from her unconscious action that any of her memory had returned. Thank heavens.

She thought guiltily of Jordan. He would be furious with her if she gave herself away. But if she did…she would want him with her. Protecting her.

She pivoted as though she had intended to find the rest room all along.

She also found an unoccupied desk with a phone, which she used to call for an appointment with the doctor who had been recommended to her. No, it wasn't urgent, she told the receptionist. In that case, the soonest the doctor could see her was nearly three weeks away.

Good, Sara thought. By then, maybe she would have her memory back and be able to cancel altogether. If not…well, she'd worry about getting a psychologist's help then, too. Perhaps even hypnosis.

When she returned to her desk, Izzy said, "I'm going to run out and grab myself a sandwich. I'll get one for you, too, if you'd like, then spell you for a while so you can eat it."

That sounded great to Sara, who asked for a tuna fish on wheat.

A couple of uniforms sent in Code Sevens, requesting permission to go temporarily off duty for lunch. Sara had to calm an overwrought young man, possibly a teenager, who'd called in to report a traffic accident before she could get all the information necessary to send the right kind of help.

There was a call from an older woman reporting someone suspicious prowling around a vacationing neighbor's house.

And then came a 9-1-1 call that made Sara's hands go icy as she typed in the particulars.

There had been a murder at Main and Live Oak. It sounded particularly vicious.

And the murder had been committed with a steak knife.

Chapter Six

Sara went through the appropriate procedures. Coolly and dispassionately, she reported a One Eighty-seven— a murder—and sent additional black-and-whites to help secure the crime scene. She notified Acting Police Chief Carroll Heumann, who happened to be in his office—the slightly smaller one next to her father's. She called the town's medical examiner, Lloyd Pederzani, whose office also occupied a corner of the same small municipal building as the police station.

And she notified the department's head felony detective on duty: Jordan Dawes.

She hated how her voice shook as she spoke with the man who was her husband. "I—I don't know for sure if it has anything to do with my father's, or Stu's, deaths, but the murder weapon was a steak knife. June told me that's how they both were killed."

"June has a big mouth," Jordan said, "but I'm glad you know now. I take back everything I said before. I'm delighted you were dispatching today, Sara, and that you let me know so quickly what happened and made the connection. I'll head for the crime scene now." He paused and said, "I may be a little late picking you up, but just stay there, okay?"

Her heart pounded so painfully in her chest that Sara wondered if it produced a jungle beat audible over the phone. Stay here? How could she sit still anywhere?

She muttered something to Jordan that might have been an affirmative. But she didn't know what she would do.

The murderer had struck again—possibly. The same person who had killed her father, and had tried twice to kill her, too.

She wasn't alone, but neither did she feel entirely secure here, even if it was the police station, for a new shift had begun, and the people around her were strangers.

Perhaps that was only because she didn't recollect them, but they were strangers nevertheless.

The answer came to her with no preamble as another dispatcher appeared to take her place. "I guess you don't remember me from the academy five years ago, do you?" asked the uniformed man with buzz-cut blond hair who appeared to be about her own age.

At least, Santa Gregoria required its dispatchers to take some police training, Izzy had told Sara. Many jurisdictions didn't.

"I heard you don't remember much of anything," the other dispatcher continued. Surprisingly, he blushed. "Sorry, Sara. I'm Marty Lusk." He held out a hand that was clammy when she clasped it.

She quickly gave Marty a rundown on the computer screen as to which of the black-and-whites were where, which uniforms were still on duty and who she had dispatched to the murder scene.

And then she sat on the hard wooden bench meant for civilians near the small reception desk at the front of the station.

She felt exhausted. She felt frightened. Her head ached.

But she knew she could not remain there. Nor did she want to go home alone.

What she wanted to do was to visit the crime scene. See if she could help in some manner—though with her memory so unreliable, she wasn't certain how.

But she could at least see if the latest body jogged any recollection regarding what had happened when her father died.

"Anyone here have better information than this on a homicide?" An older man Sara had met at her father's funeral hurried into the room, waving a piece of paper.

"Dwayne?" she asked tentatively. She thought his name was Dwayne Gould. He was dressed in a gray jumpsuit with the words Santa Gregoria Medical Examiner's Office embroidered in red on the chest pocket.

"Hi, Sara. We got a report on a homicide from here—did you send it over?" She nodded. Dwayne continued, still sounding excited, "Dr. Pederzani will be there to confirm the death, but I'm supposed to be ready to pick up the victim when the investigation team releases the body. When I looked at the notes, I couldn't make out the location."

"Main and Live Oak," Sara repeated automatically, as she had so many times while dispatching to the scene. And then she had an idea. "Take me there with you, Dwayne, please?"

"I'd be glad to."

SARA SAT BESIDE Dwayne in the front seat of the slow-moving ambulance that bore the emblem of the Santa Gregoria medical examiner's office. Before getting into the vehicle, she'd made it clear to everyone at the station where she was going, and with whom. She also made sure that Dwayne heard her. If anything happened to her, the old man beside her would be the obvious suspect, and he knew it. She felt safe, therefore, riding with him. She doubted he was the murderer. And even if he were—he wasn't a fool, was he?

She glanced over at Dwayne, who clutched the steering wheel as though it were a rope he held to keep from falling over a cliff. He squinted toward the road, studying each turn he made.

She remembered the aging driver as having needed a shave at her father's funeral. Now his face was pouchy, though hairless. He appeared worn out, like an overused tire…all except for his eyes. They were wide. They were excited.

"Do you know any details about the homicide?" he asked in a voice that suggested that he wanted to hear everything, the grislier, the better.

Maybe *she* was the fool.

She'd felt alone among strangers at the police station, but at least there had been safety in numbers there.

Where had Dwayne Gould been when the latest homicide victim was stabbed to death?

Had he come after her the day of her father's funeral? Had he killed her father, and then tried to kill her?

But getting involved in his job didn't make the poor old man a murderer, Sara told herself. "I haven't heard much, just that the victim was stabbed," she said.

She didn't mention the steak knife that had apparently been found on the scene—and that might link this homicide to the previous ones.

"Who found—was it him or her?"

"A Latina female." She repeated the information she'd been given. "According to the person who called, the victim's body was in a ditch by the side of Main, at a vacant lot where an old abandoned supermarket was recently torn down to make room for a new shopping center."

She watched the streets as Dwayne drove. They looked vaguely familiar, though she could not be certain he had headed in the right direction.

Was her life in danger? She felt her pulse throb in her throat. She clutched a small flashlight she kept in her purse. It wasn't much of a weapon, but aimed right, it could do a little damage. She would be ready this time, just in case....

They stopped at a light. Dwayne looked over at her. "How's your memory, Sara? You got it back yet?"

She tried to compare his voice to the hoarse, disguised whisper that had demanded a similar response at the cemetery. Maybe...but she couldn't be certain.

She could protect herself best by being essentially truthful. "I really don't remember anything that happened to me, or even people I knew, from before I was hit on the head. It's really frustrating, Dwayne." She hoped she wasn't laying it on too thick. On the other hand, that was exactly how she felt.

"I can't even imagine." He shook his head so that the wattle of skin beneath his chin rippled, then turned back to his driving as the light became green.

In another minute, Sara felt relieved when Dwayne pulled behind a black-and-white with flashing lights. Several companions were parked along the curb. "Here we are," he said. "Thanks for your company, Sara."

She thanked him, in turn, for the ride. Now that they had reached their destination safely, he seemed a harmless old man, even if he were excited about his gruesome job. But, as Sara knew, looks could be deceiving.

She stood beside the medical examiner's van, looking around. The vacant lot swarmed with people who must be part of the crime investigation team—though, unsurprisingly but frustratingly, few looked familiar to Sara. The area was cordoned off by yellow tape, proclaiming it a crime scene. Outside the perimeter, people in suits spoke earnestly to others filming them with news cameras.

Oops. Sara hadn't thought of the media being here. She had been fairly successful in avoiding them before, but she certainly didn't want her presence here to reignite their interest in her father's death. Nor to link the two. That was a job for the police, if it were true.

At least she was in her uniform. For now, she would pretend to be one of the patrol officers, see if there was anything she could do to help with the investigation—and learn whatever she could.

JORDAN NOTICED SARA the moment she arrived.

He wanted to dash to her side, shake the beautiful, frustrating, disobedient female who was his wife until she agreed to listen to him, then drive her straight home.

He didn't. He couldn't stay at home to protect her, as this new investigation was vital. And if he approached her now, it would only call attention to her presence.

Instead, he kept an eye on her, all the while pretending total absorption in the conversation he was conducting.

''I'll just take a few samples here to send along to Texas, like the other cases,'' Jordan said with a polite, ingratiating smile at Carroll Heumann. They had already thrashed this out. Jordan had made it clear that, though he considered the facilities available to the Santa Gregoria force commensurate with what would be expected for the moderate size of the town, it didn't compare with the resources of the Texas Rangers.

"Talk to my new criminologist first." Heumann motioned to a young stranger who'd been barking orders to the crime scene technicians. "Dawes, this is Ben Marvin, the new criminologist I just hired from San Francisco. Now that he's here, I've decided to put him in charge of a new task force to investigate all of these homicides."

Marvin looked as if he were barely out of high school, though he had silver at his temples. He held out his hand to Jordan. "How do you do, Mr. Dawes?"

Jordan needed to get to Sara. He hadn't time for amenities.

And he didn't much like the idea that Heumann had brought in some fresh-faced kid to take charge of this particular criminal investigation. Maybe this task force was a new idea spawned as a result of the latest murders, and maybe not. Was Ben Marvin in Carroll Heumann's hip pocket? If so, what better way for Heumann to keep from getting nabbed as the serial killer?

"I'm fine, Ben," Jordan responded, shaking the kid's hand. "If you want to learn the way the Texas Rangers conduct an investigation, just ask me."

Marvin's hand withdrew as if Jordan had burned him. "No one told me—" he began.

"Meantime," Jordan continued, "I'll just go ahead and look around. Maybe offer a little guidance here and there."

Some members of the Santa Gregoria police force

might have been trained by the mighty Los Angeles Police Department, a couple hundred miles to the south, but as far as Jordan had been able to ascertain, none had the skills his Texas Ranger training had provided.

Ben Marvin might have book learning, and even a smattering of experience, but Jordan was certain *he* knew more. A lot more.

And he also had an ulterior motive: to conduct his own surreptitious investigation. He needed evidence to link this most recent homicide not only to Stu's and Casper's murders, but to all the others, as well.

What was Sara doing? She seemed intent on getting near where the body of the victim lay.

He had to spare her that.

"Excuse me," he said to a glowering Heumann. "I'll keep you informed about what I find. Pleased to meet you, Ben."

He'd learned, in the SEALs and in Texas, that he should never turn his back on an enemy poised to strike, whether it was a rattler or a foreign rebel. And as far as he could tell, Heumann could be equally lethal. As a result, Jordan brushed past the acting police chief's shoulder as if he intended to go someplace his angry superior couldn't see.

That did the trick. Heumann turned toward the perimeter of the busy crime scene, where some eager reporters took advantage of the opportunity to start hollering questions at him.

The man wanted the permanent job of police chief. He wasn't about to anger the media. Though he didn't appear pleased, he shouted promises about a press conference as soon as there was something to report. He also introduced his new criminologist, Ben Marvin.

That gave Jordan his opening to sidle off toward Sara.

By the time he reached her, she was standing over the body, which was just being covered for transportation to the medical examiner's office for an autopsy. Her face was white, her lips drawn into a grim slit, and she was trembling.

As angry as he was, he couldn't yell at her when she was like this. He took her into his arms. "What are you doing here, Sara?" His voice was cooler than he had intended, and she stiffened.

"I had to see." He could barely hear her response. "It sounded so similar to what they say happened to my father."

"Sounded?" He whispered directly into her ear. "Then it didn't jog any recollection?"

She shook her head abruptly in the negative. "It isn't fair," she exclaimed, then tried to free herself from his grip. When he looked down at her, tears flowed down her cheeks, but she dashed them away.

Several emergency medical technicians prepared the body for transportation. He gently but firmly took Sara's arm. "Come with me. Maybe something else here will stoke your memory."

For several minutes, Jordan didn't conduct his usual, thorough crime scene supervision and scrutiny. Instead he led Sara to each set of technicians who combed the area for evidence.

As they walked from one area to the other, Sara asked Jordan questions, which he attempted to answer. Maybe something would, in fact, trigger a recollection.

"Who was it?" she asked in a too indifferent voice.

"The victim was an older woman."

"I heard she was a Latina," Sara said.

Jordan nodded. "The time of her death isn't established, but as far as the medical examiner could tell, it was earlier today."

"A knife killed her?"

There was a tremor in Sara's voice, and Jordan clutched her hand harder, pretending to help her over some flat earth on the vacant lot that she was unlikely to trip over. "That's right."

They learned from a couple of the technicians that the cause of death appeared to be the severing of a vital artery. The ground was soaked with blood. Despite Heumann's new pet criminologist, Jordan needed to make certain that the investigation was done right. He confirmed that the crime scene was gone over thoroughly and professionally. Photos from all angles were already being taken. At his direction, the area would be scoured for footprints and other physical evidence— especially items that might contain fingerprints. Scatter patterns, if any, from the blood would be noted. The dirt would be analyzed to determine if another blood type mingled with the dead woman's. An autopsy would be performed, and samples would be taken to see if she had fought back and gotten her assailant's skin or hair in her hands or beneath her nails. If any trace of the attacker was located, DNA analysis would be performed to try to establish identity.

"And the murder weapon?" Sara asked Jordan. "Was it like the one that killed my father?"

"Not identical," he said gently. "But similar enough to show the signature of the same killer."

She pivoted to face him. "And Stu—he died the same way, didn't he?" Her voice rose. "I wish I could remember."

"It's all right, Sara." Jordan pulled her close, laid

his cheek comfortingly against her hair—and found that her soft, sweet body pressed against his gave him immeasurable comfort, too. She smelled like lemonade and reminded him of summer days in his childhood. "You don't have to remember," he told her, knowing his tone was too harsh.

"Tell me about the knife, and how many other people have been killed the same way." She didn't let up, this fragile but tough woman he had married for all the wrong reasons...though he had considered them right at the time.

He kept his arms wrapped around her. "I don't want to get into it here, Sara, but there has been a serial killer loose in Santa Gregoria for several years. I'll tell you more later."

"No," she insisted. "Now. I won't keep you from your work here. Just explain quickly how this is all related. You can fill me in on more details at home tonight."

Jordan almost smiled. Whether or not she remembered, this was the Sara he had married: forceful, single-minded and determined. He had found her as sexy as all get-out then, even though she'd been off limits.

And now she was also fragile, vulnerable...never mind the way his groin tightened and his body ached from touching her. Even if she didn't realize it, she was *still* off limits.

"All right," he said, releasing her. Telling her what she wanted would have to act as this moment's cold shower. "I'll explain more later, but here's a rundown. In these serial killings, the murderer's method is always the same—multiple, deep wounds from a very sharp steak knife, which is left near the body. The knife is always a common type, one available in dozens of discount or kitchen stores. It never contains fingerprints. The penetration depth, location and angles of the wounds are always similar enough to indicate the same perpetrator. That information hasn't been provided to the media, so it's unlikely to be a copycat. There were about four deaths before Stu's and two after—not counting Casper and this one.''

''And the serial killer even goes after police? That's foolish,'' Sara said. She paused. ''Or maybe not, since he or she hasn't been caught yet.''

''That's the thing of it.'' Jordan couldn't keep the frustration out of his voice. He grasped Sara's arm enough to start her moving toward the curb where a group of investigators and others appeared to have gathered for a conclave. ''There was a discernible motive for the perpetrator to kill Stu and Casper, who were closing in. But there is no pattern whatsoever to the other murders—at least none anyone has figured out so far.''

''Then this poor Latina woman—''

''Is the first and only Hispanic. There have been middle class and affluent white people and an African-American doctor, and none have been killed at the same time of day or in similar locations. Nor is there a set time between the killings. Except for Stu and Casper, they appear to be utterly random.'' They had reached the perimeter of the group. ''And there's more that I'll tell you later,'' Jordan said.

SARA SQUARED her shoulders and followed as Jordan jostled his way into the crowd of law enforcement people. Her mind was whirling with all he had just told her.

The only people who formed any pattern in the serial killer's victim list were her family members.

She undoubtedly was being saved a place of honor on that list.

But she didn't even know who to be afraid of. If only she could remember....

Standing together were Carroll Heumann, who appeared to be leading the discussion, several uniforms including June Roehmer and Ramon Susa, the medical examiner, Lloyd Pederzani, and even Dwayne Gould.

Jordan had suggested that Stu and her father believed the serial killer was on the Santa Gregoria law enforcement team. Could the murderer be right here? She looked from one face to the other. Most were beginning to look familiar now. Was one the serial killer? She certainly couldn't tell by anyone's appearance.

"All right," Heumann was saying. "I'm going to leave a team of uniformed officers here to ensure that no one disturbs the site. Meantime, the techs will continue to collect evidence under the direction of Ben, here." He gestured toward the young criminologist who had been introduced to Sara.

She had assumed that Jordan was in charge of the investigation, but Heumann wasn't acting that way. And Ben Marvin looked more uncomfortable than effective.

"Has anything helpful been found?" Jordan asked. Though his expression was grim, he didn't question Heumann's apparent withdrawal of his authority.

Heumann shook his head. "Only the usual. The knife, multiple stab wounds, lots of blood. Far as we can tell, there's nothing extraordinary on the victim. Not even any defense wounds on her hands. The hairs we've removed from clothing appear to be all hers. But the lab'll check on that, of course.''

"Is the victim ready to be transported?" Lloyd Pederzani asked. "I've got a driver here ready to go." The medical examiner nodded toward Dwayne Gould.

"I'll check. You gonna do the autopsy yourself?"

Lloyd nodded. He was dressed in a jacket similar to the jumpsuits worn by the technicians, with a logo on the pocket. His hung on him, making his face appear even more gaunt. "With this high profile a case, I can't trust it to one of the part-time staff." His frown made his face sag.

"Is it okay if I get the EMTs to put the body in my ambulance and get on my way?" Dwayne asked his boss, who nodded. Dwayne dug into his pockets and pulled out his car keys as he started to walk away.

"How long before we'll have some results?" Heumann asked Pederzani.

But Sara hardly heard him. An eerie sensation of terror crept up her back. What was causing it? She looked around again to the people with whom she stood.

She met June's eye. "Are you all right, Sara?" the female officer asked. She looked concerned as she took a step toward Sara.

It was Jordan's arm, though, that kept her from sinking to her knees. He hadn't been that close to her, or so she'd thought. But she leaned into his welcome support.

"I'm fine." She made her voice as strong as she could as she lied through her teeth. She was anything but fine.

"Did you remember something, Sara?" asked Ramon Susa. He looked concerned, too.

In fact, as Sara glanced at each member of the group, what she saw written on all the faces was concern.

She didn't need Jordan's gentle pinch beneath her arm to remind her of the necessary answer to Ramon's question. "No," she said with a sorrowful yet decisive shake of her head. "I still don't remember a dratted thing."

Chapter Seven

The scream woke her.

Her eyes popped open. She gasped into the darkness, groping around for blood, for her father's body. All she felt was clean, dry linen. She was in a bed. Her bed.

Only then did Sara realize that, this time, the scream had come from her.

She heard the pounding of footsteps in the hallway. The door burst open and she saw Jordan standing there. He was backlighted, his tall, broad form silhouetted by the bright light in the hall that poured in around him.

His Beretta was in his hand, pointed upward; his other hand steadied his elbow.

"Sara? What's wrong?" He didn't wait to find out. He flicked on the light and the sudden brightness made her blink. He strode into the room, his back against the wall, then pivoted, his gun still aimed toward the ceiling—but Sara was certain that he was poised to use it if necessary.

Which it wasn't. "I had a nightmare," she said in a tiny voice that she immediately reviled. She cleared her throat. "I dreamed about my father's death."

In an instant he'd put the safety of his gun back on, and laid the weapon on the floor. Then he sat beside her on the bed. He wore only a pair of dark plaid boxers. "Did you remember anything?"

She sighed, trying not to stare at his very masculine, contoured chest. "I think so—but nothing very useful. There was something...a sound, I think. I heard it, and then I saw a figure without a face. I saw the knife in his hand—"

"His?" Jordan demanded. "Are you sure it was a man?"

Sara hesitated, then shook her head. "No. It happened so fast. My father dove toward the...person, just as whoever it was shoved me hard against the wall. The pain was excruciating, but it didn't last long. And...that was all."

"Do you remember why you went to that hotel room? It was the one reserved for your father to get changed in before and after the ceremony."

Sara thought about the question. "No, I don't. I still don't remember everything that happened in that room, or even before." She felt tears rush to her eyes. "I don't even remember our wedding ceremony."

She wanted to huddle into a miserable little ball, but Jordan didn't let her. He reached out and grabbed her shoulders with his strong, broad hands. "It's okay, Sara. You'll remember everything in time."

"I...I guess so."

She thought about it, and the silence lengthened. She was aware that his hands remained on her shoulders. Her legs were beneath the sheet and blanket, but the air was cool, and his touch warmed her—all the more because she realized she was wearing a silky golden nightgown that she had picked out specially before she went to bed, just in case this was the night Jordan decided to come to her.

And he had. Just not for the reason she wanted. Although…maybe she could turn her nightmare into an opportunity.

She straightened slightly, then gazed into the depths of his dark blue eyes. She couldn't remember if she'd ever been much of a seductress, but she tried to instill all the sultriness she could imagine into her smoldering look. "Jordan," she whispered, then let her eyes rove down his all-male body.

He was beautiful. His muscular form could have been sculpted by the most skilled of artists. His pectoral muscles appeared firm, his arms thick and powerful, his stomach washboard-perfect. She reached toward him, let one hand gently stroke the center of his chest, where just a smattering of wiry hair grew.

And she could not help looking below. There was a bulge in his boxers that told her he was as aroused as she.

Why, then, did he let go of her and stand as if the bed had suddenly caught fire—and not with their burgeoning sensual awareness?

Confused, embarrassed, she turned away. "I'm sorry, Jordan," she whispered, unsure what was happening but feeling mortified by her own rejected forwardness.

"There's a lot you still don't remember, Sara." His voice was flinty, but she detected a hoarseness, as well.

She glanced at the clock. It read three o'clock. "We don't have to be at work for hours yet," she said as conversationally as she was able. "Maybe this is a good time for you to tell me everything."

SHE WAS RIGHT, Jordan thought. But he took his time dragging a chair from another room into her bedroom.

By then, she was sitting on the corner of her bed and had wrapped a fraying black terry-cloth robe around her—thank the Lord.

But even something as shapeless as that failed to hide *her* shape. He had nearly lost all control before, seeing her lovely bosom rising and falling beneath that clingy gold nightgown, feeling her heated stare on him, her hands touching him, her sweet citrus scent....

Now, he had thrown on jeans and a white T-shirt. He slammed the chair he carried onto the floor, but the sound was muffled by the deep navy plush carpeting. Sara's room seemed to fit her, with its maroon and blue decor, feminine but no nonsense. The only furnishings were her teak bed and matching dresser and nightstand. She had a small office down the hall.

"Okay, Jordan," she said, "tell me everything." She glanced down at the bed beside her. "Unless you're afraid to be alone with me in a bedroom when I'm not screaming." Her words taunted, but he could hear the hurt behind them.

"Would you rather go downstairs? I could make us some coffee."

"No need on my account," she said. Her large hazel eyes regarded him expectantly. There wasn't a hint of the sensuality he had seen in them a short while earlier...and he missed it, dammit all! Even with no makeup, her black hair mussed around her pale face, she was a beautiful woman.

And it was all he had been able to do before to keep from ignoring every feeble ounce of conscience he had and accepting her generous, sensuous invitation.

"It was your father's plan," he began with no further preamble. "Your brother Stu was murdered three years ago." He glanced at her, and she nodded. This part of the story she had heard since she'd lost her memory. "Casper believed it was the work of a serial killer who had started murdering people in Santa Gregoria a year or two earlier. Casper only recently found some notes of Stu's that supported a very believable theory that the killer's involved in law enforcement in Santa Gregoria."

Again, Sara nodded. "Stu's...murder—" she stumbled over the word "—had the same signature as the other killings, you told me that at the crime scene." It was a statement, not a question.

"That's right. It appeared random, not tied in time or place to any of the previous ones. Despite his suspicions, he had somehow been taken by surprise, so there were no defense wounds on his hands. But he was repeatedly stabbed by a sharp, otherwise ordinary steak knife that was left at the scene. Same angles, same stab locations as prior—and later—killings." Jordan watched Sara grow even more ashen, her pale lips opened, then partially closed as she bit her lower lip. "I'm sorry," he said gently. "I'm talking like a cop, not a friend."

"A...a friend?" she said. Her eyes widened, and he thought he saw a dawning dismay.

"That's right," he said. "As I told you, I was Stu's friend from our Navy SEAL days."

"And I had a crush on you," she finished with a wry smile.

Startled, he asked, "Do you remember now?"

She shook her head, and as her black hair skimmed over her shoulders he had an urge to run his fingers through its silkiness. *Stow it!* he commanded himself, clenching his fists.

"No," she said. She sounded regretful.

"Anyway," he continued—maybe just a little regretfully, too— "Stu and I kept in touch. You got married."

Sara stood up so fast that she grasped the bed to keep from falling. "I'm married?" She appeared horrified. "I mean, to someone other than you?"

"Not now." He grinned at her. "Don't look so scared. No, you're divorced, Sara. I can't tell you the particulars. No one related them to me. But they must have been pretty bad, since when I came here you told me you were willing to go along with your father's scheme because you had no intention of ever marrying again for real."

"You mean—"

There was no way of softening it. And so, looking straight into those lovely, fearful hazel eyes of hers, he said, "That's right, Sara. You and I married at your father's request—to catch Stu's killer."

SARA FELT as though one of those ugly little steak knives was pressed against her own gut.

"Then it was a sham of a marriage?" Her voice was little more than a whisper. She took a deep breath and sank back onto the bed.

"No," Jordan said. His Texas accent was a little more pronounced, the way she'd noticed it turned whenever he talked about difficult things. "It was a very real wedding ceremony. According to Casper, it had to be. It was the only way he could think of to bring me here without arousing the perpetrator's suspicion."

"I see." Sara felt as though she were treading water in an icy mountain stream. "To ask a Texas Ranger just to come here for a long visit would have been pretty obvious if the killer's a cop, too."

"Exactly."

Jordan sounded relieved that she seemed to understand, but when she glanced at him, his eyes, beneath their prominent brows, had grown an even deeper blue. They studied her, as if trying to ascertain whether she was going to laugh—or throw herself out a window.

She had no intention of doing either. "So I agreed to a marriage that…what? We would end as soon as we caught the killer?"

He nodded. "Your brother's notes showed that he'd been collecting evidence for a while, though it was still pretty slim, which is probably why he hadn't discussed it with Casper. But the killer must have known Stu was on his…her…trail and killed him. When he found Stu's notes, Casper did some additional investigating on his own but didn't come up with much. That was when he called me, told me what he had in mind. I thought it was too bizarre, but I agreed to come here to talk to him—and to you, since he'd already gotten your concurrence." He lifted his hands, palms out, in a plaintive gesture. "It was hard to resist when the two of you ganged up on me. I caved."

His brows raised in anticipation, as though he waited for her to holler at him about his part in the ridiculous plan. And it *was* a ridiculous plan—although she could see why her father had come up with it. And, maybe, even why she had gone along with it, if her real first marriage had been that terrible.

But— "So why did you agree to it?" she demanded of Jordan. "Why on earth would you marry a…friend, just because that friend's father asked you to?"

"For Stu's sake," he replied simply.

And that explained it all. This man was a Texas Ranger. From what Sara knew of them—another strange recollection, when she could remember so little of her own life—they were dedicated lawmen and skilled investigators and, at least theoretically, had high integrity. Jordan was also a former Navy SEAL, and the combination proclaimed his courage.

His good friend Stu had been murdered, and he had agreed to a particularly harebrained scheme to catch the killer.

Only the killer had struck again and had murdered Jordan's main cohort in his plan: her father, Santa Gregoria's chief of police, who had requested his help.

"June told me Dad and you argued at the wedding."

"That was part of the plan. In-laws bicker. An elite investigative team setting up a sting doesn't."

Sara believed him. He had married her as part of a well-strategized scheme with her father that had gone awry.

Now he was stuck with only her.

"Are you going to leave now?" she asked. "My father's not here to help with your plan."

"I'm staying till I succeed," Jordan asserted in a tone that seemed to dare her to kick him out. His scowl was equally fierce. "There's even more reason for me to be here with Casper gone. I'm going to catch his killer, Sara—his and Stu's. Believe me."

"You blame yourself for my father's death, don't you?" Sara asked quietly, studying his tortured face. He didn't answer. He didn't need to. "You shouldn't, you know. It was Dad's own plan that got him killed."

It was easy enough for her to say. But it was clearly much harder for Jordan to accept. He didn't respond.

"Okay," she continued. "I'll remain your cover, if you'd like."

"You're sure it's all right?" He spoke in a monotone, as though her reply didn't much matter to him. She suspected that just the opposite was true.

"Sure it is." Sort of. She wanted the creep who'd killed her father and brother caught, too. And if that meant staying married to Jordan...well, it was, she supposed, the least she could do.

At first, of course, she hadn't even remembered that they were married, let alone why they were married.

And she had practically thrown herself at him.... "I'm really sorry about what happened earlier, Jordan. I didn't mean to make you uncomfortable."

"I didn't mind," he said, finally relaxing. He even grinned suddenly and unexpectedly. He put his hands behind his head as he leaned back in the chair. Heavens, even though she knew now that Jordan hadn't married her for love, or even for sex, he still could stoke her inner fires just by a casual motion that flexed his powerful muscles.

She felt herself flush. "In any event, now that I understand, you won't have to worry about my coming on to you anymore. In fact, I'm sure I won't have the slightest interest in you, that way."

He slid forward on the chair again and muttered something. It sounded like, "I wish I could say the same thing."

"What?" she asked.

This time, when he looked at her, all trace of humor had once again abruptly disappeared from his face. Instead, his eyes seemed to captivate hers and penetrate through them to her soul. Heating her. Melting her.

Causing a sizzle inside her that she tried hard, after all this, to douse with chilly thoughts.

Unsuccessfully.

"Don't look at me like that, Jordan," she ordered, only her voice held no conviction.

He was suddenly beside her on the bed. His arms were around her and he whispered against her lips, "Why not? We're married."

"But you just explained—"

He nibbled at the corner of her mouth. Her eyes closed and she inhaled slowly. She caught the scent of him—a trace of the soap he had showered with earlier, a hint of leather, and a healthy dose of man.

"Now that I've explained," he said, "I won't have to worry about taking advantage of you. You know the whole situation. If we both, willingly, choose to enjoy our enforced closeness—well, we're adults. We can make up our own minds." As he made this speech he ran his lips down her jaw, along her neck, and right to the sensitive skin at the very top of her breasts. On the way, he had pushed down the top of her robe and the nightgown underneath.

She sighed, allowing herself to enjoy the sensation of having Jordan Dawes kiss her. Seduce her. Love her.

Only—

He wasn't loving her. And she certainly didn't love him—did she? Their marriage had just been a business proposition. Just because she had once had a crush on the man didn't mean that, before she'd lost her memory, she'd had any feeling for him whatsoever. In fact, she doubted that she had, or she wouldn't have agreed to this cold-blooded arrangement.

And now? Now she didn't know what she felt...

except his tongue, making its way down her right breast.

"No," she said. She gently but firmly pushed Jordan off her.

"No?" he asked. He replaced his mouth with his softly stroking hand as he pulled back. His dark blue eyes were glazed with passion and the seductive expression nearly made her reconsider.

But they still had to work together. They still had to find the person who had killed Stu and her father. And sex between them would only be a distraction. Pleasant, perhaps. No, it would be more than pleasant, she was certain of it. But definitely a distraction.

"No," Sara repeated decisively.

THE EXECUTIONER, alone in the dark private lair chosen for cunning and secrecy, was not happy this morning. Usually, sleep came with no difficulty, particularly after a perfectly planned, perfectly performed assassination, such as the one accomplished yesterday.

Yet The Executioner was uneasy. Sleep had hardly come the night before. And that caused an anger so great that it felt like time to kill again.

Quickly.

That could be dangerous, of course. Especially since there had been so little time between the execution of Casper Shepard and the latest subject.

But danger was an important part of The Executioner's approach.

The executions had always been set at intervals to appear random. That had always led to much time in between. It showed The Executioner's patience.

It was part of The Executioner's plan.

But patience was wearing thin now. And there were

too many extraneous forces at work. Forces that could drive The Executioner to feel concern about getting caught.

That meddler, Jordan Dawes, for example. He had come here to marry pretty Sara Shepard. The business of Stu's sister, Casper's daughter, should have made little difference to The Executioner, for Sara's work on the Santa Gregoria police force was simply routine. She had presented no danger...before.

Jordan Dawes, on the other hand, had been a Texas Ranger. He was pushy. He insisted on taking charge.

And that could not be. He would need to be stopped.

As would Sara.

Sara claimed to have no memory of the execution of her father. Her memory might never return.

And yet...could that chance be taken?

No need. Sara would make a sweet subject of an assassination, very soon.

It would be additional revenge on Stu and Casper. It would teach a lesson to Jordan Dawes. Perhaps it would even convince Dawes to return to the Rangers, where he belonged—after sufficient time had elapsed for him to grow resolved to never catching the person who had executed his darling wife.

In the meantime, The Executioner could lay low, plan and enjoy a rest.

A well-needed rest, especially after the previous night.

Oh, yes. The Executioner would act again, and soon. The purpose was plain, and only then would peace be achieved.

The next execution would be different, of course, as they all were. And this one would be particularly fun.

The Executioner would toy first with the subject…and therefore with all those who intended to stop the executions. That would never happen.

And Sara Shepard Dawes had to die.

Chapter Eight

Sara couldn't imagine that she would fall back to sleep that night, but she must have, for when she awakened light was streaming through a gap in her blue-and-burgundy-print curtains.

Pretty curtains, she thought idly. They went well with the rest of the decor of the attractive room.

Had she decorated it herself?

She began to sigh, and in the act of inhaling smelled the fragrance of coffee.

Coffee? She put her robe over her nightgown in preparation for going downstairs, then thought better of it. Last night, her ratty-looking robe had been no deterrent to Jordan's sex drive.

Or, truth be told, her own.

But now that she knew the facts, knew their wedding was a sham, she would simply have to keep her lust for Jordan in close check—though she couldn't believe that, even if she had her full memory, she would ever have met anyone as sexy as him.

She pulled on blue jeans and a loose U.C.L.A. sweatshirt, ran a comb through the tame waves of her black hair, then went downstairs.

Jordan sat at the butcher-block table, staring at the

mug clasped between his hands. His eyes were at half mast, as though he hadn't slept at all.

Good, Sara thought. Out loud she said, "Good morning, Jordan. I hope the rest of your night was as refreshing as mine." She threw him a grin that grew all the wider as he frowned sidelong at her, then blinked.

She went to the Mexican-tile counter at the room's perimeter and poured herself a mug of coffee from a half-full carafe. Then she joined Jordan at the table. He wore a dark blue shirt that she figured must have done a fantastic job of complementing his eyes, when they weren't bloodshot.

She considered teasing him further, then decided against it. "I didn't get to sleep all that quickly last night after you left my room, Jordan," she said seriously. "I thought a lot about what you said."

For the first time his eyes widened, and he shot her a seductive leer.

"Not about *that,* though that was part of it." Sara felt redness creep up her face. "I was considering our plan to catch the serial killer." She hesitated. "So far, I think the score for the latest round is killer two, good guys zero."

"Mm-hmm." Jordan's response sounded affirmative. He took a sip of coffee, then, as if it had finally awakened him, he added, "Any ideas how to even the score, coach?"

"Even it? No way! We need to win."

He smiled then, revealing his white teeth. Lord, the man was sexy even when he looked as if he needed to sleep for a week. His light brown hair was mussed, as if he hadn't bothered to comb it after an unsuccessful attempt at sleep. His slightly bent nose added to his ruggedness. He needed a shave.

Sara had an urge to scratch her fingertips along his rough cheeks. Instead she clutched her coffee mug as if it were the stubborn rudder on a wayward ship.

"Any suggestions on how we play the game next?" Jordan asked.

"Well, we…" Sara's voice trailed off. "I guess I didn't approach this right, did I? It's not a game. Not at all."

"No," Jordan agreed. "It isn't. But any investigation involves strategy, Sara. Your father's strategy was to get me here to help, since I've developed an expertise in investigations over the years, especially in the couple I've been with the Rangers. I started training some of the Santa Gregoria technicians in more modern techniques even before…before we got married. Thanks to your dad's planning, I came here a month early to join the Santa Gregoria police, help with wedding plans, that sort of thing." He shook his head, sadness suddenly washing over his craggy face. "I hadn't thought the techies would need to implement the new techniques so soon—not once, let alone twice. And certainly not in the investigation of Casper's death."

Sara tried to hide her wince as she stood and walked toward the kitchen's center island.

"The killer is smart, though," Jordan continued. "Too smart. There's been no physical evidence left at any of the sites but the signature knife. Soon, though, a mistake'll be made. It has to happen. The killer will get too confident."

Sara put her mug on one of the decorative tiles, then fidgeted with its position. "I have an idea, Jordan. One that will mean we don't have to wait for a mistake that may never come."

"Why do I get the idea that I'm not going to like it?"

"Maybe because I turned my back on you."

"Then turn around, Sara, and tell me face-to-face."

That wasn't really something she wanted to do. On the other hand, she had concluded before that, memory or not, she was a relatively brave person. Otherwise, she wouldn't have liked herself much; she was certain, at least, of that.

She spun so her back leaned against the counter, then crossed her legs, feigning nonchalance. She doubted she fooled Jordan. She certainly wasn't fooling herself. "Okay," she said, spreading her arms out as though in capitulation. "Here I am."

Again the expression on his face indicated he was recollecting where they'd been heading last night until Sara had put on the brakes. He seemed to be considering her invitation. This time, Sara met him lusty stare for lusty stare.

Jordan laughed. "All right, Sara. Enough of this. Tell me your plan."

"It's simple, really. I'll just let it be known that my memory is coming back. Whoever killed my father won't be pleased. He—or she—will figure I'm a threat and come after me. Meantime, you'll be guarding me. So will others on the force. I'll be fine, the killer will be caught, and you can go happily home to Texas." She forced a smile onto her face. She hated the idea of Jordan going back to Texas. Leaving her.

Because she would be totally alone, she told herself. She remembered no one from the past, and her father was dead now, along with her brother.

But she would survive. Without Jordan...

She turned and grabbed up her mug again. She prepared to stalk back across the kitchen for a coffee refill when she felt two strong hands grab her arms.

She was turned with a roughness she hadn't anticipated. Those dark blue eyes of Jordan's radiated fury as he glared down at her. "That is the most ridiculous, asinine, foolhardy scheme I've ever heard of, Sara Shepard."

"Dawes."

Confusion softened his glower just a little. "Yes?"

"Not you. Me. You forgot the 'Dawes' at the end of my name."

"I did, didn't I?" Jordan's voice was no less forceful. "And that's all the more reason not to do something so stupid. I won't jeopardize my wife's life for a harebrained—"

"Wife in name only," she reminded him.

"It doesn't matter. You won't be the bait in the trap, Sara Shepard *Dawes,* and that's final."

"Nothing is ever final, Jordan," she contradicted. "Not till death."

"Or until I've said no, Sara," he said ominously.

"And have you said no, Jordan?"

"Yes."

"Which is it, yes or no?"

Sara knew she shouldn't be taunting him this way. His expression blazed—was he that angry? He still held her arms, and she thought he was going to shake her.

But...the blaze wasn't rage. Not entirely, at least. His eyes narrowed and one corner of his mouth pulled up in a quirky smile. "No, Sara," he said gently. "You are not going to do anything foolish...except kiss me."

He didn't allow *her* the chance to say no. Instead he bent and covered her mouth with his own.

She was glad that he still gripped her, for her knees went suddenly weak. Maybe it was because of the molten lava flow inside her, for he used his lips and tongue to simulate the most erotic of sexual acts, and she nearly wanted to cry with need for him. "Jordan," she whispered against him. "We're not really married."

"Sure we are." His reply was a sensual hum against her ear. "It was a real ceremony. Your father insisted on it."

"But…" The mention of her father brought Sara up short. She pulled her head away from Jordan's questing mouth, though that didn't stop him. His lips merely roved down her throat. "Jordan, please stop. Real ceremony or not, we never intended it to be a real marriage. I didn't like marriage, remember? You told me so yourself."

"Ah, but that wasn't with me." His hands had gone behind her back and were molding her buttocks through her jeans, then downward between her thighs. She felt a hardness pressing against her stomach and inhaled at the sheer carnality of what Jordan was doing to her.

"Then are you willing to make it a real marriage?" she managed to ask. "Are you willing to stay here forever with me, as my husband, Jordan?" *She* didn't want that—did she?

She didn't know *what* she wanted. Wouldn't, until her memory returned.

But suddenly that answer was the most important thing in the world to her.

And it came quickly, as Jordan's talented hands left her body. Left her bereft, needing something she would not get. Not now, and not later.

"No, Sara," he said roughly. His breathing was

hard, and it was his turn to lean against the center island. "I thought you understood. This…marriage was to be a temporary assignment. I've gotten a leave of absence from the Rangers. When I'm done here, I'm going back." He looked her straight in the eye. "Alone."

A SHORT WHILE LATER, Jordan watched Sara's lithe form move gracefully from the refrigerator to the stove, then back again. She was preparing eggs and bacon for their breakfast. It was a beautifully domestic scene—but he knew that, simmering below her poised surface, was a well of hurt.

He hadn't intended to hurt her earlier. All he had wanted, at first, was to make it clear that she wasn't to put herself into jeopardy for the sake of catching the killer.

Further jeopardy, for she was already in danger. The person who had murdered her father, right in her presence, might not believe that Sara truly had amnesia. Or might be—justifiably—worried that her memory would come back.

Sara didn't need to taunt the killer with that.

Just as she didn't need to taunt Jordan with her damned sexiness. But that, at least, was unintentional—at least, he believed so. Every move she made, every look she gave him, made him want to drag her to the floor and make long, lustful love with her.

But she had taken him aback with her earlier question. Was he willing to stay forever with her? Make their marriage, arranged by her father, into a real one?

He took a quick swig of the now tepid coffee in front of him, wishing it were laced with something stronger. Heck, no! was the answer.

If they both agreed to enjoy its physical benefits in the meantime, fine. But permanence? Never. He had a life in Texas, with the Rangers, and he fully intended to return there.

Besides, how could he stay with Sara, when her father's death was his fault?

"Wheat toast or white?" Sara asked, interrupting his thoughts.

"Wheat. You're sure I can't help?"

"There's nothing left to do, Jordan." She turned her back on him again.

Nothing, he thought, except to catch a killer. And to find a way to keep his hands off Sara while they worked together and lived together. Did everything together—except what he wanted the most.

THAT MORNING, Sara had a hard time staying awake at her post as dispatcher. So far, it had been a pretty slow day: the routine communications from cops checking in and out, a couple of 9-1-1 calls that turned out to be about minor traffic accidents, plus a purse-snatching at a local restaurant where a couple of irate patrons had caught the thief.

A foam cup sat beside Sara on the large, crowded table that held her computer and all the radio and telephone equipment of her job. She'd felt comfortable enough to go refill her coffee twice, sure she wouldn't be late in answering a call.

"Hi, honey."

Sara looked up to see Jordan standing above her. He had dressed earlier in a dark blue shirt and black trousers, and he looked wonderful in them. She, of course, was wearing her uniform on the job.

"Hi, sweetheart," she replied in a syrupy voice. She

cringed internally, though, at the public reciprocal endearments, knowing how hypocritical they were. Jordan might like her as a kid sister. Maybe even as a potential bedmate—though he could wait until the full moon actually sank screaming into the Pacific before she would let that happen.

Even if the recollection of how close they had come last night still made her tingle all over.

She liked him, of course, the way any woman would appreciate a fine work of masculinity. Otherwise, they were simply two near strangers on a mutual mission.

"Everything all right here?" Jordan asked, leaning over to snoop into the notes she had taken about her calls that morning.

"Just the way it should be," she replied. "Quiet."

"Good. I wanted to let you know I'm off to the lab to see some stuff from yesterday's crime scene. I've already told some of the guys around here to keep watch over you while I'm gone." He gestured around the crowded station, where nearly every cubicle was staffed by a uniformed cop talking on the phone or writing a report. The place smelled like coffee and the mints some people ate to hide cigarette smoke on their breath.

"You just worry about yourself, sugarplum," she said with a broad smile—enjoying *his* wince. "I can take care of myself."

"I'm sure you'll do just fine someday," he said with his perfect white teeth gritted. "When you get your memory back. If you ever do." Each word came out precisely and a little too loudly, just in case someone around them was listening.

Sara wanted to add another sarcastic retort, but the

admonishment in his eyes made her reconsider. She might not like it, but he was right.

For now.

She gave an exaggerated sigh. "I sure hope it comes back soon," she said in her own slightly raised voice. "This is just too frustrating."

He bent and planted a kiss on her lips that she felt clear down into her comfortable regulation shoes. "See you later, Sara."

"Yeah," she said, wishing she could convince her body as easily as her mind to ignore Jordan Dawes. "See ya."

Later that morning Sara was relieved from duty for a fifteen-minute break by a female cop named Aloise, who she didn't remember meeting before. Sara wanted to use the opportunity to ask a few questions about the investigation of the two recent murders, but on wandering around the station, didn't find anyone she remembered meeting before.

She used the break to jot down a bunch of questions that had come to her mind and to pour herself more coffee.

She thanked Aloise and settled back down to what she hoped would be the continuation of a routine morning.

A couple of Code Seven messages came in: two pairs of patrol officers wanting food breaks. Since both units were in the same area, she typed into the computer an authorization for a break for one car's occupants and directed the other to wait.

"Hi, Sara. How's it going?"

She turned to see Lloyd Pederzani standing there. The medical examiner wore a brown plaid suit jacket that hung on his thin frame, and a flowered necktie.

"Fine," she replied.

He gestured to a chair on wheels near hers. "Looks like things aren't too busy now. Do you mind if I sit down?"

She smiled at him, recalling how he had come to her hospital room and cheered her with jokes. But he didn't appear to be in a joking mood now. His gaunt features appeared a little troubled and very sympathetic. Sara had a feeling he had something to tell her, and she wasn't sure she wanted to hear what he might have to say.

But better sooner than later, she supposed. "Please do."

Before he sat, he came close to her and peered at the area where her bandage had been days earlier.

"How's your head?" he asked.

"The sore spot's nearly healed," she said, "though it's still a little tender when I touch it."

"Any headaches?"

Sara hesitated before answering.

Lloyd pulled his pant legs slightly and sat in his designated chair. "Sorry if I seem nosy, but like I told you before, I've been a friend of your family's since way back. We've been too close for me to be your family doctor, but I was always interested in your dad's health. Yours and your brother's, too." He paused. "I guess your memory hasn't come back yet, has it?"

She shook her head slowly. "Not really. Every once in a while I get a twinge, as if something's trying to come to the forefront of my mind, but almost nothing has."

His sad eyes seemed to light up. "But some things have? If so, that could be a good sign." His smile was pleasant but gave his face an even more horsey appearance.

"Maybe." She sighed and turned back to her computer screen. She was still on duty and could not allow herself to become distracted, even if she kept their conversation brief. "Still, it's been nothing of significance."

And if it had been, she wouldn't feel comfortable telling Lloyd, even though he appeared good-hearted.

And although he didn't present the same town-wide broadcast system that June Roehmer did, Sara knew better now than to trust anyone here with any secrets. Especially people affiliated with law enforcement—as every one of her acquaintances seemed to be.

The local medical examiner might only be peripherally involved with the police, but he was still a close associate with the department, called to many crime scenes and in the thick of many felony investigations, including assaults and homicides.

He was a practicing doctor, as well, she recalled. "Do you know much about amnesia?" she asked. "I mean, in your experience, do most people who get it recover their memories fully?"

He shrugged his bony shoulders. "I don't have any actual experience of the problem to draw on, Sara. My expertise is internal medicine. Though in some ways that involves a lot of different medical fields, I don't feel qualified to do much with neurological and psychological areas. I've never had a patient with amnesia. I could ask some colleagues, though, if you'd like."

She shook her head. "Don't bother. I quizzed the specialists at the hospital and they were both encouraging and discouraging. Every case, they said, was different."

She glanced over at Lloyd. He was nodding sympathetically. When she looked back at her computer screen, she noted that the officers she'd allowed to take a food break were going back on duty. She typed in permission for the other unit's occupants to take their break.

When she was done, Lloyd said, "I didn't mean to take up so much of your time, Sara. I just wanted to let you know that my lab has sent its final report on your father's death over here to the police department. I don't imagine it's something you'll want to bother with, but you might tell Jordan it's arrived. I'm not sure what the politics are around here these days, but I know your acting chief seems to think that leaders don't have to be team players. He isn't always forthcoming in giving information, like what's in that report, to people he considers to be his troops."

"But Jordan isn't just another detective," Sara protested. "He's got special training as a Texas Ranger." And he intends to catch this particular killer, Sara thought.

Lloyd put up one thin hand. "I know that and you know that. And, I'm certain that Carroll Heumann knows that. But Carroll's bucking for the appointment as permanent police chief to succeed your dad. He seems to consider your new husband a thorn in his side, so he might try to keep him out of the loop on these serial killings. That way, if the crimes get solved, the success won't be attributed to Jordan."

"I see," Sara said. "Thanks, Lloyd. I'll tell Jordan. Is there anything in the report you think I should be particularly aware of?"

Lloyd opened his mouth as if to speak, then hesitated. "Well, I guess the most significant thing is that it fits the serial killer's pattern. Same kind of stab wounds as those incurred by your brother and some of the other apparent victims.'' He touched Sara gently on the shoulder. ''But maybe that is information you really don't need to know.''

''I do *need* to know it,'' Sara said around the lump in her throat. ''Even if I don't *want* to know it. Thank you.''

''My people are just finishing the autopsy on the latest victim. I'll probably bring it around later today.'' Lloyd excused himself then. ''Don't ever hesitate to get in touch with me if there's something I can do to help you, okay, Sara?''

''Sure, Lloyd.'' But she was already preoccupied, for her phone was ringing. It was a 9-1-1 call about a bank robbery in progress.

She did her job well, she thought, calling out all units in the area. Some of the other police officers at the station gathered around her to listen in to what was happening. Within a half hour, the robbers were thwarted and caught, and no one had been hurt. Sara sat back at her desk and smiled.

But almost immediately another call came in on a general line, not 9-1-1.

''Santa Gregoria Police,'' Sara said in her most crisp professional voice.

''Sara?''

The voice was so low that Sara wasn't sure she had even heard her name.

''Excuse me?''

''Sara,'' the voice repeated just a little louder. It was high-pitched and slightly garbled, as if the speaker had swallowed helium before talking.

''This is Sara Dawes.'' Her stomach clenched, but

she refused to let her uneasiness show in her speech. "Who's calling, please?"

"You know, Sara."

She felt her breathing almost stop.

The station door opened and Jordan strode in, looking as handsome and collected as ever, and Sara wanted to scream at him.

Instead she concentrated on her phone call. "Who is this?" she demanded more forcefully. Her screen already showed the location from which the call originated. It was a pay phone in downtown Santa Gregoria, a mile away. Would it do any good to set up an incident report, send a black-and-white? Only if she kept the person talking long enough. She checked to make sure that the equipment that taped every call appeared to be functional.

As they had during the bank robbery, people who worked at the station had begun to gather around Sara. She pushed a button to make the conversation audible. Jordan joined them. His hand was firmly, protectively, on her shoulder.

But his touch was not enough to shield her from the next words she heard from the phone.

"I executed your brother, Sara."

The whiny voice was so matter-of-fact that Sara gasped. From the corner of her eye, she saw Jordan take a menacing step toward her table, as if he wanted to attack it in lieu of the caller. She held up her hand as if to calm Jordan. "Identify yourself," she insisted, forcing her professionalism to the forefront of her mind.

"I executed your father, too," whined the voice. "Can you guess who's next?"

Jordan's mouth opened as if he were going to respond, but Sara beat him to it. "You're next, you dirty—"

"You have to catch me first, Sara," said the voice. "How's your memory? Has it returned yet?"

"N-no," she stammered. "But it will someday, and when it does—"

"What did you think of my little execution yesterday, Sara? It must have reminded you of your father's. You looked so sad."

"Then you were there!" she said triumphantly. Stu had been right. The murderer was someone connected with law enforcement, probably crime scene investigation.

"Maybe, maybe not. I like to admire my handiwork, but sometimes it's smarter to stay away and let a picture or two say a thousand words."

"You planted a camera?"

"Did I say that? In any event, Sara, I'm watching you. Your memory will return, and when it does, you'll die. But first, I'll kill your meddling husband."

Sara looked frantically up toward Jordan. He shook his head slowly and smiled at her, as if in reassurance.

But she was not reassured. And the voice hadn't stopped.

"Only your husband is not very smart, Sara. I'm much smarter." The voice paused for just a moment, then said, "Beware!"

There was an eerie, shrieking laugh, and then Sara heard a click.

Chapter Nine

"Wait!" Sara shouted. "Don't you hang up on me, you SOB." She stopped. She had used a masculine epithet, yet she still hadn't been able to tell if the killer was a man or a woman.

And who was to say that the caller was actually the serial killer? It could have been a crank.

A crank with an awful lot of information.

"Did you see where it came from?" Jordan demanded. "Have you sent a patrol car?"

"Yes," Sara said weakly. The officers reported in a minute later. No one was at the pay phone, which was in a secluded alcove in a bustling downtown Santa Gregoria office building.

"W-what do we do now?" Only when she spoke did Sara realize her teeth were chattering.

Jordan must have noticed, too, for she was suddenly enfolded in his arms. She pressed her cheek against his chest, wishing that, for now, his sympathy was not just for show here, at the police station where they both worked. That he really did care for her, as he would an honest-to-goodness, forever-after wife.

And then she recalled how caring he had been after she had been attacked and her father killed. They were alone part of the time. Jordan had been kind to her and compassionate. That must simply be part of who he was.

And it would do her no good—no good at all—if she allowed herself to fall in love with him because of his endearingly masculine and protective personality.

No more good than if she let herself fall in love with him for his sexiness.

Falling in love with Jordan Dawes could be fatal to Sara's sense of well-being.

"You're going to be fine, Sara," he whispered into her ear. "I'll make sure of it. Don't worry."

Her sense of well-being was just fine here, held close in his arms, despite the terrible things that despicable person had said to her over the phone. But she couldn't stay here forever.

She pulled away. "Of course I'm fine," she said. "But we have to catch whoever it was, Jordan." She looked around. Cops from all over the station were hovering around them, looking angry, uneasy.

Strangers. Not one of the friendly faces she'd learned to recognize as belonging to special friends was among them.

But they were still her co-workers and cohorts. They would stick by her.

"Look, everyone," she said, "I wish I could remember what happened when I was hit and my father was killed. But I don't. If any of you has any suggestions how to catch this creep, let us know, will you?"

An affirmative murmur circulated through the crowd. A man in uniform with the name M. Herbert on his ID pin stepped forward. "You up for a twenty-four-hour guard, Sara? Even if the chief—acting chief—won't authorize it, I'll bet we can get up enough volunteers for a watch like that.''

Sara felt tears fill her eyes. ''That's a wonderful idea. And maybe I'll take you up on it. Let me think about it.''

Of course, Sara still believed that the killer was in law enforcement. She might only make it easier for him—her—to get to her if she agreed.

Jordan must have had the same concern. ''I like that idea, Mike, except that it's reactive instead of proactive. We'll keep an eye on Sara, that's for sure, but we also need to gather enough evidence to discover this creep's identity. Haul him in before he can hurt Sara or anyone else, ever again.''

''Yeah,'' sounded a chorus around them. But no one else offered any suggestions.

''Just think about it,'' Jordan said. ''You come up with any ideas, let me know.''

''Tell you, and not Heumann?'' asked Mike with a grin.

''Our illustrious acting chief probably won't be happy about it,'' Jordan acknowledged. ''But it's not his wife who's been threatened. You can always tell us both. Just tell me first.''

That elicited a laugh from the crowd, which began to disperse.

Sara sat on her chair. She looked up at Jordan and said in a shaky voice, ''Speaking of our acting police chief, Lloyd Pederzani was here. He told me he'd brought a lab report that compared my father's wounds with those of other victims. He wanted me to tell you, in case Chief Heumann forgot to.''

''Thanks.'' He squeezed her shoulder, then said, ''I'll be right back.''

When he returned a minute later, he held a thick report in his hands. "This is it," he said in a low voice. "I'll have a copy made for me, but in thumbing through it I don't see any surprises. We were already fairly certain that the modus operandi in all of the killings was similar, and this just seems to confirm it."

Sara nodded—just as a phone rang. Iciness crept up her spine. She didn't want to answer....

"Do you want me to get it, Sara?" Jordan asked.

His question spurred her to action. "It's my job," she said, and reached for the receiver. She was proud that she kept the quiver out of her voice.

It was a 9-1-1 call from a cell phone. There had been a major accident on Route 1. Police, fire and EMT crews were needed immediately. "I'll get someone there right away," Sara said, and leaped into action, using her computer and microphone to get black-and-whites and others on their way, doing what she had been trained to do.

Doing what she now *recalled* she had been trained to do, which made it all the better.

It also helped her state of mind when she finally had a moment to breathe and look up. Jordan was still standing by her table, leaning on the nearby wall, his muscular arms crossed. A smile was on his face—was it one of pride?

"You do your job well, Sara Shepard Dawes," he said.

"You remembered the Dawes this time," she noted.

"I certainly did."

"IF THERE WERE any place I could put you that I'd feel you were safe, you know I'd do it, don't you?" Jordan glared from the driver's seat of his car toward Sara, who was in the passenger seat.

"Do you really think I would stay, just because you put me there?" His wife's scowl was no less irritated than his own. "I need to go back to the crime scene, too, Jordan. The person called me on the phone, not you. Suggested that he or she might not even have been present to get all the detail described, hinted at a camera. It's important to me to help check it out."

"But it could be dangerous. The killer might have alluded to additional evidence to get you back there. Maybe he wants to start a new signature, murdering all his victims in that particular ditch—including the one person in the world who has the best chance of identifying him."

"Or her." Sara nodded pensively. "That's true, I suppose. Maybe there is a camera, maybe not. But in any event the whole call could have been designed to lure me there again."

"Right!" Jordan said triumphantly. "And that's why I need to find someplace safe to plant you while I check it out."

"On the other hand, the caller threatened you, too, Jordan. It might be you he or she wants to draw back there. That means I need to find someplace safe to plant *you*—"

The car stopped, and her words were cut off by Jordan's mouth on hers. She tried to shout, "What are you doing?" but nothing came out. It was very clear what he was doing—and her traitorous lips were responding. Not only that, but her entire body wanted to get into the act.

If they hadn't been in the car, she might have embarrassed herself and joined in the seduction.

At least, she noticed when he let her come up for air, he'd had the presence of mind to pull over to the curb.

She glanced around. Of course he'd pulled over. They were at the corner of Main and Live Oak...the scene of yesterday's crime.

She folded her arms belligerently. "Don't do that again, Jordan. It won't work. I'm going to help you investigate."

"Do I have a choice?"

She ignored the sidelong look of wry amusement in his all-too-sexy eyes. "None at all."

"Then stay right beside me, Sara. Pretend we're literally joined, and not just in matrimony. At the hip. Stuck with permanent glue. Got it?"

She felt her chin raise as she gave him an arch look of her own. "That's fine with me," she said. "That way I can make sure nothing happens to *you.*"

"Sara." He dragged her name into several syllables, his tone admonishing. "If anything dangerous happens here, I want you to listen to me. Run if I say to, hit the dirt, whatever."

"Absolutely, Jordan," she said with a challenging grin. But then her smile faded. "Jordan, when the call came in before..." Her voice trailed off.

"Were you wondering who it could be, who wasn't at the station?"

She nodded.

"I was, too. Unless something pops up to convince me otherwise, I have to assume Stu and Casper were right—that our perpetrator is affiliated with Santa Gregoria law enforcement. The lack of physical evidence confirms that it's someone who knows what he's doing. Most of the guys around during your call were uniforms, cops I don't know well. Cops who didn't seem particularly close to your father, either, and some are too new to have even known Stu.''

Sara nodded. ''Once we've looked around here for a camera, I'd like to go back to the station, ask a few innocent-sounding questions about where everybody was at the time the call came in.''

''You'll let me ask those questions, won't you?''

''Of course, Jordan,'' Sara said sweetly.

THEY FOUND NO CAMERA, or even anyplace where one could easily have been hidden and removed. It was just as Jordan had suspected. The lot containing the ditch where the body had been found was practically leveled. It was in a busy commercial area, where someone was sure to have noticed a camera mysteriously being placed, although the lot itself wasn't much frequented. No one had found the victim's body for a day or so.

The closest business to the empty lot was a single-story dry-cleaning shop. The owner said that he had security cameras inside his establishment, but hadn't any on the exterior. Nor had he noticed anyone appearing to install a security system anywhere in the neighborhood.

The responses of the manager of the barber shop down the street and the owner of the two-story antique shop nearby were similar. There was an oak tree on the antique shop's lot, and Jordan climbed it, looking for any indication someone had hung something in it. He found nothing—except that Sara's eyes seemed to be watching him much too admiringly as he swung himself down. Her intense and hungry look made his groin tighten. And that made him irritable.

''Nothing here,'' he snapped as they walked back to

the car. "Your call was probably from some kook who just wanted to get a rise out of the police."

"Something got a rise out of one particular policeman." Sara's tone was a touch too innocent. He thought her gaze was trained on the ground, but then she looked up at him sideways and he knew she had been studying him. And that made him rise all the more.

Damn! He had known from the beginning that this assignment would be tough. He was supposed to find out who had killed one of his best and oldest friends. It required an honest-to-goodness marriage ceremony, for a fake one would have fooled no one in Santa Gregoria law enforcement, certainly not the murderer.

But he'd had no inkling of how difficult it would be to keep the marriage from being solely in name only.

He no longer wanted to keep his hands off Sara. He wanted to protect her—and he wanted to make love to her till neither one of them could move. The two goals were not compatible. He knew it. And Sara had suggested that the only way she wanted sex was if it went along with forever.

That couldn't happen. Therefore sex couldn't happen.

Why was it so hard for him to get his traitorous body to understand that?

WHEN THEY GOT BACK to the station, Carroll Heumann had returned. So had June Roehmer, Ramon Susa, and other uniformed cops whose shift had just ended.

Jordan had already thought of how to interrogate those who'd been out in a way he hoped was subtle enough to prevent hackles from being raised—since to him, everyone around here was a suspect until the killer was caught.

Sara, still determined to participate in the investigation, stayed at his side. She was a distraction he didn't need, but he knew by now that he wasn't going to convince her to let him pursue the perpetrator alone.

He went into the briefing room where the uniforms just relieved from their last shift had gathered.

"Please sit there," he told Sara, designating the end seat in the first row. She seemed uncharacteristically meek as she obeyed, and he wondered what mischief she had on her mind. But as he got up in front of the group, she merely watched attentively. He wanted to take that beautiful face of hers in his hands and pull it close—

With difficulty, he dragged his concentration back to the group in front of him. He told the cops all about the phone call Sara had received, then said, "I'd like a written rundown of where everyone was from ten-thirty to eleven o'clock this morning, what pay phones you might have passed, if you saw anything suspicious. The computer equipment seemed to have a small problem so we're not sure it pinpointed the right pay phone." He felt Sara's surprised glance but didn't look at her. "It seems fine now, at least. Anyway, if you split up from your partner, let me know that, too, even if you just went to the can for a minute. One of you might have passed the right phone at the same time the other was ordering his Big Mac."

"You want us all to write a separate report?" asked Ramon, sounding displeased. His uniform shirt was now unbuttoned at the collar, and he ran his hands through his short, dark hair.

"You have a better idea?" Jordan replied. Did Ramon object because he didn't like writing reports—or because he had something to hide?

Ramon Susa had been on the force for four years, according to his personnel file. From what Jordan had gathered, he'd come from a difficult background in Simi Valley, near L.A.: his father had deserted the family when he was a kid, his mother made ends meet any way she could, including from men for sexual favors. Ramon had gotten in trouble with the law as a kid but a kind cop on his local police force took him in tow and straightened him out.

Maybe. Or maybe the young cop had simply hidden his true colors when he joined the police in Santa Gregoria.

Rumor had it that he'd argued with Stu before his death. Had it been an everyday, innocuous misunderstanding—or a prelude to murder?

Ramon was now June Roehmer's partner. The small, pixie-like female cop sat beside Ramon, and she leaned over to him now, engaging him in conversation.

Jordan also considered June a suspect. Sara was right; the killer could be a woman, and June was certainly strong enough. Despite her size and deceptively innocent appearance, she bested three-quarters of the men in hand-to-hand, self-defense training. Plus, she had been dating Stu Shepard before he was killed, and Casper had kept in close contact with her. What if she had used her familiarity to set them up, if they had been getting too close to catching her?

As Sara's friend, June might now be doing the same with her.

Jordan scowled, then caught Sara's questioning gaze. He shrugged and said, "Are we all clear on these reports now?"

June asked, "How about if partners write just one report together but submit separate pages for the times they were apart? I gotta tell you that Ramon and I spend a lot of time together, but potty breaks are definitely separate."

That got a laugh from the others in the room that seemed to end abruptly.

Jordan looked around. Carroll Heumann had walked into the briefing room. "What's happening here?" the stocky man demanded.

Jordan explained what he had just requested.

"Waste of valuable time," Heumann rumbled, glaring at Jordan.

"Maybe so," Jordan replied, "but I'd like you to do the same kind of report, since I'm also trying to determine what areas of town might not have been covered by police presence during the phone call."

"Who gave you the authority to demand such a thing from anyone, let alone me?" Heumann's challenge was reflected not only in his words but in the furious look that narrowed his small eyes even further.

"It's my fault." Jordan looked down to see that Sara was now at the front of the room with them. "The call really scared me, Carroll. And then the computer malfunctioned—a power surge, maybe. The screen went blank for a split second." She gave the older man a look through her eyelashes that made Jordan's blood start pumping double-time, even though it hadn't even been directed at him. "Since we couldn't be sure where the call came from, Jordan and I talked about other ways of finding the caller and this seemed to be the best idea—at least it's a process of elimination. It would really help us. And it shouldn't take a lot of time. In fact, I think it's a great idea if people who were together submit joint reports to save time.''

And to make it clearer who would provide alibis for one another, Jordan thought. Maybe he should have been irritated with Sara for her interference, but instead he wound up smiling at her for her ingenuity in attempting to convince Carroll Heumann, while at the same time reinforcing Jordan's request to the others.

He just hoped that none of the officers gathered around at the time of the call contradicted them about the computer malfunction. He'd brief Sara later about making sure she said it happened several minutes after everyone had stopped milling around her, just in case.

"Please, Carroll," Sara repeated.

The look Heumann turned on Jordan suggested that the acting police chief wasn't fooled about the reason for the report. Still he said, "All right. I'll do a quick write-up. In fact—Sara, you come into my office and I'll dictate my report to you. You can type it up on your computer—as long as it's working now.''

"Sure thing, Carroll," she said, but she rolled her eyes when she looked at Jordan.

He wondered whether Sara's being alone with Heumann was a good idea. The acting police chief was at the top of Jordan's suspect list.

Not that Jordan had any evidence against him...just a gut feel. Something about the man wasn't right. And Jordan's gut seldom steered him wrong.

But Sara should be safe with him here, at the station. And maybe she could get something interesting out of him—a confession?

Keep dreaming, Dawes, he told himself.

"Oh, Jordan, here you are." He looked toward the

door to see Lloyd Pederzani, the medical examiner, standing there.

"I'm through here," Jordan announced to the roomful of cops, then headed toward Pederzani.

He wasn't surprised to be joined by both Heumann and Sara.

"I saw the report you brought in earlier," Heumann said to Lloyd, "but I'm still waiting for information on that latest autopsy."

"I saw the other report, too," Jordan said. "Thanks for letting me know it was here, Lloyd."

Heumann shot a scowl first at Jordan then at Lloyd.

Pederzani's long, gaunt face lightened. He wore a short-sleeved white shirt fastened tightly at the collar, and a striped necktie. "Well, I do have that autopsy report with me. But maybe I should just give it straight to Jordan this time, since he has special expertise in investigations."

"I'm still in charge." Heumann stared challengingly at Pederzani.

The thin medical examiner just shrugged. "I thought your appointment as acting chief was only in effect till someone else was chosen by the mayor and city council?"

"Yeah," Heumann acknowledged, "but I intend that it'll be me."

Lloyd Pederzani's sparse eyebrows lifted questioningly. "Really. How interesting." He didn't sound as if he believed that the selection was at all a shoe-in, which seemed to rile Heumann all the more. "Anyway, poor Casper hired Jordan, and I, for one, am glad. He can look into these serial killings with a fresh eye—and the perspective of a Texas Ranger."

An ugly red crept up Heumann's fleshy face. "I

could've assigned him patrol duty," he said, "or even fired him, but I chose not to."

"Very wise." Pederzani smiled ingratiatingly, but Jordan wasn't any more fooled than Heumann seemed to be. "Well, here are the results of the autopsy on the last poor victim, the one from the ditch." He put the report right into Jordan's hands. "Happy reading," he said, then sighed. "It all sounds so familiar now. Our serial killer needs to add a little more originality."

Sara, who stood between Jordan and Lloyd, sighed deeply. "He's already done that, Lloyd. Now he's making threatening phone calls."

Lloyd's eyes widened. "To who?"

"To me." Sara knew her attempt at a smile was flimsy.

Lloyd turned to Jordan. "With all the newfangled electronic gadgetry around here, can't you catch the miserable fiend?"

"We're working on it," her husband said grimly.

AND THE CREEP had made another threatening phone call, though Sara didn't discover that until Jordan and she had returned home. There was a message waiting on the answering machine.

Sara stood by the small phone table in the living room and pushed the button. Immediately the room filled with the highly disguised voice she had hoped she would never again hear. She sagged against the wall as she listened.

"Sara? Oh, I know your loving husband will hear this message, too, but it is especially for you."

"That's the same voice." Sara tried to make her glance at Jordan appear less terrified than she felt, but knew she failed miserably.

Jordan's dark blue eyes were narrowed in fury. He stood in the doorway, filling it with his large, stiff presence.

"This is your…friend. Just call me 'The Executioner.' I know you did not find the camera at the latest crime scene. Maybe there was one, maybe not. In any event, your efforts to find me remain inept. You will never catch me. You can be certain of that."

Jordan took a step toward the machine as though he had every intention of throttling it, absent the menace who referred to him or herself as The Executioner. "And you can be certain we *will,* you—" Jordan broke off what he was saying as the voice continued.

"I have already left a new little present. A different place, of course. And again, very soon after my latest efforts. Maybe I will rest for a year or two and then come straight after you, Sara. That's the fun of this all, isn't it—the unpredictability? Just wait and see, Sara…and be afraid."

That was the end of the message. Sara stood beside the telephone table, staring at it unseeingly. She was shaking all over. "Leave me alone," she whispered.

"He will, Sara." Jordan's voice was utterly certain, utterly reassuring. But she wasn't reassured.

"No," she said, getting hold of herself. She had to be strong—and realistic. "The Executioner won't leave me alone. That's because I won't leave The Executioner alone, either. I want the rat caught, Jordan. Now. Before anyone else is killed." She hesitated, then said in a small voice, "Before *I'm* killed."

She was suddenly enveloped in Jordan's strong embrace. He whispered against her hair, "I've an idea. Let me take you to Texas, Sara. I'll leave you with some very good friends there, also Texas Rangers, and their families. They'll take care of you while I come back here and run that Executioner thug to earth.''

"You've been threatened, too," Sara reminded him, speaking into his chest. "I'll only go if you come, as well."

"I can't do that."

"Then neither can I."

She expected him to let go of her then, in punishment for what he undoubtedly considered her stubbornness. Instead he held her all the tighter.

It felt wonderful being so near him—as though they were actually married. But she was growing too dependent on him in too many ways, and now their proximity was for all the wrong reasons. And so Sara tried to pull away.

But Jordan didn't let her. His mouth swept down to capture hers. She sighed into his potent, searching kiss, returning it. Reveling in it.

What would happen, she wondered suddenly, if she simply let herself go, enjoyed this one fleeting moment with Jordan? To fly with sheer physicality, and not worry at all about the wisdom of what she was doing.

For despite everything prudent and sensible that she had advised herself, she was falling in love with her husband.

Warmth filled her as she strained upward in his arms, trying to rain as many stimulating kisses on his face, his neck, his throat, as he gave to her. Her eyes were closed; she relied almost totally on her senses of touch and smell. The masculine aroma of him was sweet and pungent, and utterly stimulating.

"Sara," he murmured. "Oh, yes, sweetheart." This time there was no audience to his endearment. He wasn't simply trying to soothe her because of her memory loss.

Might he really care about her?

As he slid his hands under her shirt, she felt him unclasp her bra. Her breasts sprang free, and in moments they were enveloped by his warm, sensuous touch. She gasped in pleasure as he took her nipples between his fingers and rolled them gently. She no longer wanted to stand there, in her living room. She wanted to be in her bedroom—their marriage bedroom—both of them naked and exploring one another. Loving one another.

"Upstairs, Jordan, please," she whispered. He was running one hand under her uniform skirt, between her thighs, and she thought she would faint from the sheer sensuality of it.

She reached out, too, and located the bulging hardness hidden by his slacks. She heard his gasp, and then her hand was captured in his. Stopped.

She opened her eyes. His were open but glazed. He breathed deeply and erratically. "Are you sure, Sara?" he asked. "You understand that, if we make love, it's because we want to for now, and now only."

Of course she understood. He had made it clear enough before. But his reiterating it now, combined with her foolish notion that she might be falling in love with him, made it all the more unequivocal. And hurtful.

And then there was her even more foolish thought that he might actually care for her.

She inhaled as if she had been suffocating. "I do understand, Jordan," she said in as matter-of-fact a tone as she was able. "It's not that, by making love,

I'd ask for forever from you. But I don't think we should complicate things further this way. Thank you for stopping.'' She smiled her gratitude to him.

But inside she was weeping.

Chapter Ten

"I did a lot of thinking last night," Sara told Jordan the next day over a breakfast of cereal and coffee.

His glance was leery, as if he expected her to chastise him for his nearly uncontrolled lust the previous night.

But how could she blame him? She had nearly been carried away by desire, too.

That was exactly what she needed to discuss with him.

"The thing is," she said decisively, moving her gaze back to her cereal bowl, "though I still don't remember, I gather it was a three-way decision that you and I should marry, that we were all concerned it would put the killer on guard if you'd just shown up as a Texas Ranger and begun asking questions. Right?" She had racked her brain nearly the entire night, trying to remember that, trying to recall any significant people or events from before the blow to her head. But she still couldn't force even the tiniest recollection that hadn't already come to her.

And that frustrated the heck out of her.

Jordan nodded. "That's right. Your father was especially worried about tipping off the killer, and what he said made sense. Of course, Casper could make the weakest argument seem extraordinarily strong.''

Sara especially wished she could remember her father, and not just what he looked like in a photograph…or lying there lifeless on the floor beside her.

He sounded as if he'd been a remarkable man.

I will remember, she told herself fiercely. But she wouldn't worry about that now. She still had something to discuss with Jordan.

She had dressed with care that morning, though she didn't want it to look that way. She didn't go on duty for a few hours, and there was nothing alluring about her old U.C.L.A. T-shirt thrown over worn jeans.

But speaking of alluring…

Jordan had taken a seat beside her at the kitchen table. His light brown hair was damp from his shower and he looked freshly shaved. He appeared awake and refreshed this morning. Even fully dressed in a long-sleeved shirt, he was the most sensuous man Sara could imagine.

And that was why she had to get him out of her house. Soon. For unless she did, they were going to go too far one day. She wouldn't stop him, he wouldn't stop her, and they would wind up making love… something he clearly would regret afterward.

And she? Well, it was probably better if she didn't find out.

''The thing is,'' Sara continued, ''you're here now. It no longer matters why the killer thinks you came. Our Executioner knows that you *are* here, and that you're after him or her. Maybe a legitimate wedding was necessary at first, but it no longer matters.''

''Sure it does,'' Jordan retorted. ''If you think I'm

just going to walk out now, leaving you vulnerable to that piece of garbage, you're wrong." He clutched his spoon by the handle as if it were a weapon he planned on wielding if she contradicted him, and she gently reached over, took it from him, and placed it back on the table. She smiled at him—and his glower segued to a grin in return.

A too sensuous grin.

Sara bent over her own cereal bowl, holding her dark hair away from her face. This was harder to say than she had thought. "Jordan, it's just that—"

"Just that we have a hard time keeping our hands off one another."

Sara looked up at him with her mouth open, but he waved her comment gently away.

"*I* have a hard time keeping my hands off you." His slight Texas accent seemed exaggerated as he spoke. "It's me, and I admit it. You're a beautiful woman, Sara. You drive me nuts for wanting you, and that would be the case whether or not we were married. But I'm hanging around you, whether you like it or not, since it's the only way I can be sure to keep you safe."

"But—"

"Sara, sex obviously means more to you than quick satisfaction. You deserve the kind of loving you want, from a man who'll be there for you when you wake up in the morning, and every morning from then on. That's not me. When things are finally sorted out here, I'll be gone. For now, I won't leave you alone, but I won't take advantage of you, either. Okay?"

It wasn't okay. The problem was that, despite all of her own self-admonishments and great advice, she wasn't sure she didn't want to take advantage of *him*. To create a delicious memory now, by making love with him, so that, even if her earlier memories never returned, she would have one extraordinary recollection to clasp to herself.

For she knew making love with Jordan Dawes would be more than memorable.

But she could hardly make him a party to her ambivalence. And so she said, "That's fine, Jordan. We'll just make a pact to stay far away from one another."

"Okay," he said.

IT WAS SIMPLE ENOUGH to agree to stay away from his wife, Jordan thought as they drove to the station a while later.

Much harder to carry through. Though it was, of course, the right decision.

But even in her uniform, designed to be somewhat unisex and certainly not sexy, Sara Shepard was an utterly desirable woman.

Sara Shepard *Dawes,* he reminded himself. As if he had to. He kept playing games in his mind, as if by pretending he had never married Sara, he could make his promise to stay away stick.

"Jordan, should we tell anyone about that phone message yesterday?" Sara had turned toward him in the car, her lovely dark brows furrowed. "Maybe we should even have our home phone tapped so that if any other calls like that come in, they can be traced."

"I'm way ahead of you on that," he told her. "I was going to let you know later, but I've already requested a tap."

She had said it was *their* home phone, not just hers. Why did he like the sound of that? He was nuts. He reminded himself quickly of his real life—his enjoyable, uncomplicated, single life as a Texas Ranger.

He didn't even want to contemplate anything else.

Except…except their enforced nearness was making him much too fond of Sara. And it wasn't entirely due to how sexy he found her.

But he had no intention of falling in love with her. None at all. That was never part of Casper's plans, or Sara's, or his own.

"Don't talk about the message for now, Sara," he cautioned her. "If our perpetrator is one of the people who hangs out at the station, it'll only make him think we're worried."

"I *am* worried." Sara's tone was troubled.

He had pulled up in front of the thirties' vintage beige stucco station. He grinned at her wryly. "So am I," he told her sincerely, "but we don't want to give our Executioner the satisfaction, do we?"

"No," Sara agreed, and hopped out of the car.

"ARE YOU GETTING a break at lunchtime?" June Roehmer asked Sara later that morning. "I came in a little early to do some paperwork. Boy, am I swamped. I'm usually busy, but today's a real mess. Anyway, I thought we could grab a bite together before I go on duty."

"Sounds great."

Sara had been having a pleasantly slow day at her dispatch station. Most messages were from officers checking in. Only one 9-1-1 call had come in, and that was about yet another minor traffic accident. She'd had a lot of time to think. It might feel good to be around talkative June for a while to get her mind off her problems…and Jordan. No, *including* Jordan, and his unmitigated sexiness.

"I should be relieved in about half an hour," she told June.

"Great. I'll come by then." June swung around so quickly that her pixieish blond hair bobbed around her face. She hesitated, then turned back. "Have you gotten any calls or letters or... I mean... Look, Sara. You can confide in me. Is there anything new about the serial killer—your dad's death, and the rest?"

That was a strange question, coming from June. Sara had discussed possible suspects with Jordan. Sara had thought it ludicrous at first that he had included June on the list. But now...?

"Why would you ask about any calls, June?" She pivoted in her chair so she could regard the uniformed officer squarely. How about vicious telephone messages? Did June know about the one Sara had received? If so, how?

June's small mouth narrowed into a worried line. "It wasn't anything, really. Not at all. I just...something came to my attention so I thought I'd ask."

"What came to your attention?"

"I can't really tell you." June appeared highly uncomfortable. "I promised."

"It was a promise you shouldn't have made," Sara said, "but if you don't want to tell me, you should tell Jordan."

"Oh, no," June said quickly, then grew uncharacteristically silent.

That made Sara all the more suspicious. "Why not?"

June glanced around. None of the cubicles located near the dispatch station were occupied. She wheeled a chair over and sat close to Sara. "It's *about* Jordan, Sara."

A stab of fear shot through Sara's chest. "Is he all right?" She hadn't seen him since they had first come in together that morning. She thought he'd gone to the coroner's lab to discuss the latest test results with Lloyd Pederzani.

"I—I suppose so." June seemed taken aback. "That's not what I meant." She leaned even closer to Sara, who could smell her light floral perfume. "You've got to promise you won't tell Ramon."

"That depends." This all seemed terribly mysterious to Sara. She needed to get to the bottom of it.

"The thing is, he needs some time. He's trying to figure out the right person to give the letter to, since Jordan seems really involved in the investigation, and Ramon doesn't think much of our current fearless leader, Acting Chief Heumann."

"What letter?" Sara demanded in a quiet but forceful voice.

June sighed. "Ramon received an anonymous letter." She hesitated. "Sara, do you remember that, before your wedding, your father and Jordan were arguing?"

"That's what you told me."

"You still don't remember? Anyhow, Casper apparently really didn't want you to marry Jordan and even at the last minute he was trying to get the wedding called off. They were hollering at one another. Your dad even threw a punch, though I don't think he intended that it connect. Jordan blocked it anyhow. But they looked like they wanted to kill one another."

"I see." Sara dragged the words out contemplatively. But she *didn't* see. June's comment made no sense whatsoever. It had been Casper's idea that Jordan and she marry—hadn't it?

Sure, Jordan had said he'd argued with her father as part of the plot—but to *fight?* So realistically? What had really happened?

She had only Jordan's word for it.

But she trusted Jordan.

Should she trust Jordan?

June waved her hands in the air as though wanting to wipe out her words, but she said anyway, "I'm sure it's ridiculous, but the letter claims that Jordan killed Casper, then committed the other murder afterward to cover it up, make it look like the work of the serial killer."

"That's nonsense," Sara said. Why would Jordan have come here to marry her if it hadn't been part of a plan to catch the killer? He clearly didn't love her— no matter how she was coming to feel about him. He would have had no reason to kill her father, let alone anyone else.

But Sara's poor mind was growing so muddled that she could hardly think. Pain stabbed through her head, as though where she had been struck was reinjured. She touched the still sore area.

"Are you okay, Sara?" June asked.

"I think I need an aspirin."

"Maybe I shouldn't have told you. But I've been thinking about you, thinking about the situation. It's a shame. I'm really sorry."

"So," Sara said, "am I."

SARA MANAGED TO GET through the rest of the morning. It helped that only a few calls came in. At lunchtime, she begged off her proposed lunch with June, pleading that her headache was worse.

What she wanted was to speak with Jordan.

No, what she *really* wanted was her memory back, all of it. Surely what June had told her was nonsense. But she would know so for certain if she could recall her thoughts leading to her decision to go along with her father's plan and marry Jordan.

And if she could recall what had happened in that hotel room when her father was killed.

Jordan didn't come in until midafternoon, and then he was late for a meeting with Carroll Heumann. He didn't look pleased when he finally came out of the acting chief's office.

The timing worked out well, though. Sara had just started her final break of the day. She approached Jordan as he entered the wall cubicle that served as his office. "Would you come out and grab a cup of coffee with me?" she asked.

He seemed preoccupied, his brow creased in concern about something. At first he didn't seem to have heard what she'd said. And then he said, "Sure, Sara. Can we make it quick, though? I've a couple of calls to make."

"Quick is good. I need to get back for the rest of my shift in fifteen minutes. Is that okay?"

He nodded, then put his hand on the small of her back as though directing her toward the station's outer door. Sara was as aware of his touch as if it were an electrified police baton, searing his mark upon her.

She knew that was far from his intent. She walked a little more quickly until his hand dropped away.

A block down the street from the station was a Marie Callender's restaurant.

Sara recollected that several cops dropped in here for coffee and meals. She also knew, somehow, that the servers were used to providing them with quick service—and to their dashes from the place when calls came in.

As she walked through the door and inhaled the delightful aroma of baking pastry, she grinned, but hid it from Jordan. Another tiny piece of her memory had returned! Never mind that it was a small, meaningless fact; it was significant to *her*.

They were shown to a small booth in a corner, perfect for what Sara had in mind. When the waitress came over—an older woman with a pleasant face that Sara believed she recognized—they ordered coffee and a piece of French apple pie to split.

"What's up?" Jordan asked immediately.

"What makes you think anything is up?" she countered. "I only asked you to grab a cup of coffee with me."

"There's always coffee brewing at the station," he said. "And I can tell from the way you hold your mouth that you're itching to say something."

"What if I'm not?" There was no reason to bait him, but Sara wasn't sure she liked to be so easily read.

"Aren't you?" He grinned that wicked sexy grin that was beginning to make her crazy. She had to wipe it off his face.

"Yes, in fact." She waited while the waitress served their coffee and pie, then walked away. "Jordan, did my father and you actually argue about the wedding—and not just as part of your plan?"

His eyes widened so, she felt drawn into the sea-deep blue depths of them. "Who told you that?"

"Did it occur to you that I might have remembered?"

Those eyes narrowed as he appeared to try to read

the answer on her face. "Did you?" he demanded. "Is more of your memory returning?"

"No," she replied. "And yes. I didn't remember that, but I do remember small things now and then. But is it true? Did you really fight?"

Jordan nodded. "Sort of." His light brown hair, which he'd brushed back from his face that morning, was askew now, as though a breeze had blown it. But the air had been still, so Sara figured he had run his fingers through it. That signified frustration, and now she was asking questions that might spoil his mood even further.

Good, she thought. Shaking him up might get her more answers. She took a small bite of her pie, barely tasting its tart sweetness as she waited for his reply.

"He was getting cold feet, Sara," Jordan said. "We'd discussed it all for months, including the potential dangers to all of us. We all agreed the possible reward was worth all the risks, and we promised we'd all be careful and watch out for one another. I moved here, started publicizing our wedding plans, the whole nine yards, just as we'd planned. But then Casper began worrying about you."

"Me? What about himself? He was the one who got killed." Sara blinked as her eyes moistened. *Dammit, Dad,* she thought. *Why didn't you worry about* you, *not me?*

Jordan put his elbows on the table and bent toward her. His voice was even more quiet as he spoke. "He was set on finding Stu's killer, no matter the cost to himself. Stu's notes made him crazy—the ones he recently found that strongly implicated someone in Santa Gregoria law enforcement. He'd had the same suspicions, but Stu's well-reasoned ideas solidified them for him.''

"Why hadn't Stu kept Dad informed about his thoughts in the first place?"

"I asked Casper that,'' Jordan replied. He leaned back just enough to take a sip of his coffee. "He reminded me how methodical Stu was. The two of them had discussed possible perpetrators and methods to catch him, and one of the possibilities they'd come up with was someone close to the investigation. Stu had run with the idea, putting together mostly theories and thoughts, rather than provable facts.'' Jordan shook his head. "He apparently was digging for hard evidence when the killer realized it and made Stu the next victim. Your father and you only recently felt able to go through the bulk of Stu's things. He'd hidden his notes at the bottom of a box filled with old college texts and notebooks."

"I see,'' Sara said sadly. She cut another bite of pie with the edge of her fork and stared at it, instead of bringing it to her mouth. "But what about your argument with Dad? Did he really change his mind about our marrying?"

She looked up at Jordan's face and found that he looked terribly sad. "Yes,'' he said. "He became adamant at the last minute that we should call it off, to protect you. We were discussing the ramifications just before you and I actually married. He blew up, even came at me before he caught himself. I suppose it's possible that someone actually saw us.'' He stared shrewdly into her eyes. "Right?"

"Apparently,'' Sara agreed.

Jordan's broad shoulders seemed to slump in dejection. "I pushed him, Sara, because of all the trouble

I'd already gone to—and because I wanted to find Stu's killer. But I should have listened to him. The wedding was probably what led to his death. I'm furious with myself that I bulldozed him that way. Maybe if I hadn't, he'd still be alive. And the wedding certainly hasn't done either you or me any good.''

Sara felt as though an icicle had suddenly formed inside her heart and was attempting to stab its way out. ''No,'' she said, trying hard to keep her misery from showing. ''It hasn't.'' She wiped all expression off her face—she hoped—as she met Jordan's bleak gaze.

''Sara, if whoever told you about my fight with Casper was trying to convince you that I killed him, that's absolutely wrong. Do you believe me?''

''Yes,'' she said, nodding. June's mention of Ramon's letter had planted a seed of doubt in her mind. Now, though, seeing the guilt and sadness written on Jordan's face for having been so unrelenting with her father, she couldn't help but believe in him.

Yet she couldn't help feeling distressed not only that Jordan had been the one to insist that their wedding occur, despite her father's last-minute opposition, but also because of his current attitude about it.

Unless— ''Jordan, what was *my* opinion about whether we should get married?''

''You were all for it. You were determined to catch Stu's killer. Between the two of us, we finally convinced Casper.'' He sighed. ''We should have listened to him.''

Sara didn't contradict him.

Jordan glanced around, as if assuring himself that no one sat nearby. Their corner of the restaurant was practically empty. He nevertheless leaned toward Sara again and said, ''Since a little of your memory seems to be returning, can you remember why Casper and you left the reception to go to the room? Especially why you did it without telling me. We'd agreed to keep each other closely informed. Though none of us anticipated trouble on the day of the wedding, I've racked my brain and haven't been able to figure out why the two of you disappeared when you did. Do you recall why?"

"No," Sara said. "I'll think about it, but so far my few recollections have not come on demand, or about topics that I really want to remember." She looked at her watch. "I need to get back now."

He nodded. "Me, too. But remember, Sara, not to hint to anyone that even tiny pieces of your memory have returned."

"You've made that very clear, Jordan," she acknowledged dryly.

THINGS WERE QUIET when Sara returned to duty at the dispatch desk.

That gave her time to think, especially when Jordan shut the door to one of the interrogation rooms to make his phone calls. Too much time, for her thoughts roiled.

If nothing else, her conversation with Jordan convinced Sara that following his directives wasn't always in her family's best interests. Her dad had been reluctant for her to go through with the marriage. She had been on Jordan's side—though she wished she could recall her own rationale. Finding Stu's murderer had to have been paramount, but had it been her only reason? In any event, the wedding had gone forward, and the rest had become sorrowful history.

She could hardly blame Jordan for being insistent, though. Not with her own apparent stubbornness, too. And Jordan had gone to a lot of trouble to get to their wedding day—taking a leave of absence from his job, moving here, helping to put the plan in motion.

She didn't believe he'd done anything intentionally to cause her father's death. But unintentionally? That was another story.

And now—

A call came in on a nonemergency line. Sara answered.

"Sara? It's me, June. Sorry to bother you, but I've been worried about...what we talked about before." There was noise on the line as if a large truck rolled by. "I'm at a public phone outside a sandwich shop. I didn't want to use the radio, even one of the private frequencies just in case someone listened in. Ramon's gone inside to grab a drink." She paused, then said, "You haven't... I mean, you won't repeat what I told you, will you? I don't want Jordan to think badly of me."

Why was she so worried about that? Sara wondered. Unless—

Jordan had put June on his suspect list. If he thought ill of the female officer, he might investigate her all the harder.

If June were innocent, why would she care?

If she were guilty, she'd have reason to worry. A lot.

Sara decided to be honest—to a point—to gauge June's reaction. "I did talk to Jordan, told him someone mentioned hearing Dad and him argue about whether he and I should marry." Was June's silence on the other end of the phone a panic reaction, an indication she couldn't hear Sara because of the traffic that roared in Sara's ear, or simply polite listening? "I didn't tell him who let me know, though."

"Oh. That's great." June sounded relieved. "And I'd appreciate it if you'd keep it that way, okay?"

Sara mumbled something noncommittal that she hoped would satisfy June.

"I'll talk to you more about it later," June said.

"I'm glad you called in," Sara interjected, not wanting to lose the connection now—not when she could actually believe June might be the killer. She had to find out. "Can you keep a secret?"

"Sure," June said as another truck rolled by.

Sara knew she shouldn't do this. Jordan would be furious—if he ever found out.

And she would have to tell him. If she didn't, she would be putting herself in even greater jeopardy.

Don't do it, a voice inside commanded her.

I have to, she retorted silently.

Before she could change her mind, she blurted, "I'm beginning to get my memory back, June. Not everything yet, unfortunately. But bits and pieces. I'm sure it'll just be a matter of time till I recall what happened when my father died."

There was another silence, then Sara heard June talking to someone. Ramon?

She confirmed it in an instant. "Sorry, Sara. I can't talk much more now. Ramon just came outside and we need to roll."

"Did you hear what I said?" Sara had to ask. Maybe it would be better if June hadn't.

"Oh, yes," the female cop responded. "It's really, really great. I'm so happy for you! I'm dying to hear more about it. Hang around, will you? We'll talk about it if you're still at the station when our shift ends."

Sara heard June hang up. She did the same.

Oh, Jordan, Sara thought, staring at the closed door to the interrogation room. *What have I done?*

Chapter Eleven

When June and Ramon returned to the station later that afternoon, Sara took June into an empty hallway. "Now you and I both have secrets to hold over one another," she said with a laugh, hoping she sounded merry instead of scared. Could she be alone with the killer?

Was cute, pert June Roehmer, a police officer only a couple of years older than Sara, "The Executioner"?

Surely not.

But if she wasn't, could Sara trust June to keep from telling the world her memory was returning? If not June, *someone* would be very interested to hear that little tidbit of information.

June responded with a laugh of her own. "That's true. Isn't it fun?" She shook her head so the short, blond cap of her hair fluttered slightly around her face. "Anyway, congratulations. Really. Your news was so great! Does Jordan know that some of your memory is back?"

That seemed a loaded question. If Sara hadn't told her husband, that would imply she didn't trust him— as June had suggested. If she *had* told him, and anything now happened to Sara, there would be more reason for others to include him as a suspect.

She knew better, but no one else understood why Casper and Jordan had argued. Jordan would hardly have killed her father to make sure the wedding took place, not when it had been strictly a business arrangement—one more for her father's benefit and hers than for Jordan's, though they all wanted to catch Stu's killer.

"Of course I told him," Sara said, hoping her expression was that of a dreamy newlywed instead of that of a disillusioned cop. "He's concerned about my safety, if the information gets into the wrong hands."

"Oh, don't worry about me," June said. "You know me. Well...maybe you don't remember that well. Anyhow, I'll be discreet."

But suddenly a new recollection leaped into Sara's mind. It was a gruff but loving male voice—her father's? *Your young officer friend is a nice lady and, to a point, a good cop, Sara. But don't tell June Roehmer any secrets unless you want everyone on the Santa Gregoria police force to know them.*

"Right," Sara said, swallowing a groan. "Thanks."

"YOU *WHAT?*" Jordan stood so fast at the kitchen table that his wooden chair fell to the floor with a crash.

Sara winced. She looked repentant. And scared. He fought the urge to take her into his arms and comfort her.

The woman just didn't listen.

Her independence, her spirit that remained so bold and free, despite the recent loss of her father, the loss of her memory—they were all part of the package that was Sara Shepard…Dawes. A package that he found utterly appealing.

But Sara's impetuousness and willfulness had thrust her into even greater danger than she'd already been in.

"The thing is, Jordan, after our conversation earlier I'd added June to *my* suspect list, too. I wanted to find out if she was the killer. I figured that if I told her my memory was returning and then someone came after me, we'd know it was her. Only…well, another piece of memory fell into place. It could have been my imagination, but I don't think so. I've remembered now that June Roehmer is the last person anyone should trust with a secret."

Jordan let his head fall forward to his chest in his exasperation. "So if someone comes after you, it could be June. Or it could be anyone else because she told the world the 'wonderful' news that your memory's coming back."

"Exactly." Sara sounded so sad that Jordan thought she was probably chastising herself as much as he would, if he let himself.

He righted his chair and sat on it once more, facing Sara.

"So what should we do now, Jordan?"

"*Now* you ask for my opinion?" He looked her straight in the eye. To give her credit, she met his gaze head-on, though her wide hazel eyes were clearly troubled.

"I've always valued your opinion—or at least I have for as long as I can remember, even if I don't always agree with it."

"Or listen to it."

Sara nodded. "That's right." She thrust out that

small and perfect chin belligerently, as though daring him to contradict her. "I made my own decision. Now I have to live with it. If it costs me…well, so be it. But I want to be sure that, if something happens to me, you'll catch whoever it is. After all this, I don't want Stu's or my dad's deaths to go unpunished."

Or yours, came the ugly thought into Jordan's head. But that wouldn't happen. He'd already blown it once, letting Casper and Sara out of his sight on the day Sara and he were married. He would make sure she was protected, day and night—preferably by him—till the killer was caught.

Day *and* night. Could he convince her to let him stay in her room?

He felt a tightening in his slacks at the very thought.

Not a good idea. He wouldn't get a moment of sleep. He'd be acutely aware of her there with him, in the darkness, her body calling to his, whether she intended it to or not.

At least in a different part of the house, he would be able to rest—and therefore protect her better in the long run.

No, he'd stay in his own room. Or maybe even camp out in a sleeping bag in front of her door.

But stay platonically in the same room as Sara? That was torture he could do without.

AS IT TURNED OUT, Jordan got very little sleep that night.

He had decided to stay in his own room, but he insisted that Sara keep her door ajar. He left his wide open.

But it wasn't thoughts of her lying there by herself,

her curvaceous, sexy body clad in some kind of skimpy nightclothes, that kept him awake—at least not alone.

The problem was that the phone rang a little after midnight, a half hour after he'd gone to bed.

Jordan had had a phone extension installed in his bedroom. He'd told Sara not to answer any calls, in case it was the creep who'd left the message on the machine a few days earlier.

This time, the call was from Carroll Heumann. "Dawes? Take Sara and get over to apartment sixty-four in the building at Bell and Hernandez. There's been another killing."

SARA WATCHED the nearly empty road ahead of them beneath the street lamps and headlights as Jordan drove them to the latest crime scene. This late at night, the whole of the moderate-size town of Santa Gregoria appeared to exist in black and white, with some shades of gray.

But there would be red, too, where they were going. A lot of it. Sara shuddered.

"You okay?" Jordan asked. His eyes were on the road, but he must have seen her movement from the corner of his eye.

"Sure," she lied.

She wouldn't have stayed home alone even if Jordan had allowed her to. She had to be there, on the scene. To take part in the investigation, in whatever limited fashion she could.

She wasn't a trained technician, but she could at least help with any crowd control.

And Acting Chief Heumann had told Jordan to bring her. Jordan clearly wasn't pleased about that.

"At least he told you about the crime," Sara had

reminded him, fully aware of the antipathy between the two men.

Heumann had also said that this new homicide appeared to be the work of their serial killer—the self-styled executioner.

The phone message left on the home answering machine had said a new "present" had been left. This latest murder had to be it.

Sara had donned her uniform quickly. As a detective, Jordan could wear nearly anything he chose. And he'd put on an outfit that made him look as sexy as if he'd planned it: tight jeans, a blue shirt, one of his thick leather Texas belts with a silver buckle and a denim jacket that hid his shoulder holster. His badge hung from one of his pants pockets.

A group of black-and-whites, roof lights flashing, was already on the scene when they arrived. A curious crowd had gathered on the sidewalk in front of what appeared to be a three-story apartment complex in a working-class neighborhood. Area lights had already been set up, turning the night into day.

Jordan thrust his badge out the window toward a uniformed officer, who motioned him into an empty parking space near the building. Sara hopped out of the car at the same time as Jordan. She ducked under the yellow police tape and ran up the stairs into the building. Jordan was close behind; she could hear his heavy footsteps along the functional indoor-outdoor carpeting.

The crime scene was on the first floor. Some of the members of the investigative team had already arrived. Sara hesitated outside the single door to the apartment only a moment before Jordan took her hand and pulled her inside.

They entered the living room. Though the building was located in a mundane area of town and was itself ordinary-looking, the apartment was decorated with a collection of antique lamps on attractive carved wooden tables. Under other circumstances, Sara would have stopped to admire them.

"Where's the victim?" Jordan asked Ben Marvin, the town's new criminologist; Sara recognized him from the last investigation.

He had been dusting the room for fingerprints. He nodded toward an open door. "There's only one bedroom. He's in there."

He. This time, the victim was a male. Like Stu. Like her father. Like possibly two-thirds of the victims whose deaths were attributed to their serial killer, from what Sara had learned, although she, as everyone else, failed to see a pattern in the choice of victims.

"Stay right here, Sara," Jordan ordered her.

She inhaled deeply and shook her head. She edged up against Jordan and spoke so low that only he could hear. "If the signature is the same, I need to see the scene. It might jog my memory."

"If the signature's the same, it won't be pretty," he reminded her—as if he had to. She knew that. But the last murder had been outdoors. There had been a lot of blood, but scattered over a wide area.

Her father's murder—her attack—had been indoors. In a bedroom. Just maybe, if she viewed this site, she would remember something.

She reached for Jordan's hand, and he grasped hers. They edged through the crime scene crew toward the bedroom door.

Jordan preceded her into the room, then held her back. "You don't need to look at this," he told her.

She knew it must be pretty bad. But she didn't believe she had a choice. "I want to," she said.

"Okay." Jordan's voice was grim. He gripped her hand even more firmly as he led her into the room.

The familiar metallic stench of blood filled her nostrils. And then she could see the entire grisly scene.

The body was lying in the bed. Blood was everywhere: on the sheets, the walls, the pretty lamps and tables similar to the ones in the living room. Sara gasped.

From what she could tell, the victim, who had apparently suffered multiple stab wounds, was a middle-aged man with gray hair, of similar build to her father. She remembered that from seeing the man on the floor beside her, when she had awakened in the hotel room.

As her father—a vision, not just of a posed photograph but of a laughing older man with thick white hair, an extra chin, a ready grin and a growing paunch, washed over her. A man who loved Mexican food. A man who could be as officious as Jordan when the mood struck him. A man who had been there for her, no questions asked, when her first marriage had fallen apart.

She remembered her father at last. Oh, yes, she remembered.

But the memory of his murder, of the person who had killed him—it still eluded her.

"Sara, are you all right?" Jordan's harsh voice penetrated her consciousness. His arm was around her, and she realized her eyes were shut, and she had been swaying.

"I—yes, I'll be fine," she said in a shaky voice. She would tell Jordan what she had remembered, but later. Right now he had a job to do. A crime scene to investigate. And, with luck, he would find the perpetrator of *this* crime, so the other murders, too, would be solved.

"Are you Mrs. Dawes?" asked a young woman in medical examiner's coveralls. Sara didn't recognize her. "Mrs. Sara Shepard Dawes?"

"Yes, she is," Jordan answered for her, scowling at the woman. "Why do you ask?"

"Mr. Heumann told me to watch for you, Mrs. Dawes." The woman addressed Sara directly rather than responding to Jordan. "There was a note left for you here, ma'am."

Icy fingers of dread inched up Sara's back. "A note? For me?"

"Let me see it," Jordan demanded.

"We've already bagged it as evidence," the woman said. She handed Jordan a plastic bag with a single piece of paper inside.

He looked it over, then gave it back to the woman.

"Let me see it," Sara demanded. "It was for me."

"Don't worry about it, Sara," Jordan said.

"Let me see it," she repeated, holding out her hand.

His lips narrowing grimly, Jordan gave the bag to Sara.

On one side of the paper, which had apparently been folded in quarters, was Sara's name. It appeared to have been typed or computer generated.

On the other side was a note.

Dear Sara,
    This one was for you, to help you remember, since I hear your memory is returning. That is good, for you will remember me when I come for you. Do not worry, for you, it will all be over soon.

Sara succeeded in shrugging it off—on the outside, at least. Inside, she was shaking.

"I'm fine, Jordan," she told him as he took the note and handed it back to the technician. She even managed to grin at him, as though she had planned the entire thing. "Looks as if I was right. Probably due to June's blabbing, the killer has heard my memory's coming back. Whoever it is must feel threatened—and intends to come after me. We'll be ready to catch him or her then."

"Right." Jordan sounded grim. His face held no expression, but she knew him well enough to realize he was seething even more at her.

Well, so be it. Even if she had made a mistake in telling June about her memory, she couldn't take it back now. And if it was the impetus to flush the killer out of hiding—June or someone else—then Sara would be glad she'd done it.

Except…except this latest killing might not have happened if the killer hadn't wanted to teach her a lesson. She stood now along the perimeter of the bedroom. She wasn't looking directly at the body, but as long as her eyes were open, she couldn't help but see the blood. Blood that might not have been there, a body that would have remained a living person, if she hadn't—

"No," she whispered. She didn't dare let herself think that way—or she would drive herself crazy.

"No what?" Jordan demanded.

"No more staring at this gruesome scene for me." She tried to sound nonchalant but couldn't keep the quaver from her voice. "Was there… Was a steak knife found here, like with the rest?"

He nodded. "Same as always, a common brand available in most discount stores."

"Were there fingerprints on it?"

"Doubtful, though it'll be tested at the lab."

"Well," Sara said with forced bravado, "unless you have an assignment for me in here to help with the investigation, I think I'll go now."

"You can leave the room," Jordan told her, "but you can't leave this apartment—not until I can accompany you. With Heumann's blessing or without it, I intend to make sure evidence is collected right." He gently cupped her face in his large, warm hand and stared straight into her eyes. His were blank, emotionless—an expression she now recognized well. But it didn't mean he wasn't thinking or feeling; it only meant he was keeping himself tightly in check while he did what he had to.

"Sara," he continued, "I know you don't follow orders well, so I'm not telling you what to do. I'm asking you, for your own safety, to stay here. All right?"

"All right," she agreed. After all, the murder had at least partially been intended to frighten her. Why else would the killer have left her a note?

And it had succeeded. She *was* frightened.

The note might also have been intended as a trap, by forcing her to be out in public and vulnerable. If so, she had to be especially careful.

Ben Marvin had entered the bedroom and was engrossed in conversation with his two investigators and the woman from the medical examiner's office. Jordan nodded toward him. "You can ask Ben if you can help check for evidence in the living room. Otherwise, find yourself a chair in there and sit down. Okay?"

"Okay."

Marvin didn't seem pleased at Sara's request, but after a glance toward Jordan he walked with her into the living room. It was still undergoing scrutiny by two investigators who worked together as a team. Sara recognized them from the last murder scene—where the woman had been found in a ditch. After discussing it with the others, Marvin assigned Sara to label the bags containing small pieces of evidence—hair, fiber samples, even crumbs that the investigators picked up.

It was tedious work, but Sara was grateful she had something to do. Not that she anticipated that anything they found would be useful, since the serial killer had left nearly no physical evidence behind in the other homicides—no fingerprints or hair or bloody clothing…nothing except the signature knife and similar-pattern stabbings.

She watched as the others each finished going over one half of the small room, then they both switched places to double-check that the other hadn't missed anything. A third investigator was snapping pictures. He claimed he had already shot several rolls in the bedroom.

The people Sara was assisting eventually finished; most evidence to be collected was in the other room. They began collecting their paraphernalia to leave.

Sara thought of going with them, then recalled her promise to Jordan. And her own fear about what this latest murder might mean to her.

She braced herself and walked back into the bedroom.

The investigators there appeared to be far from finished. Ben Marvin was on his knees in a corner, collecting evidence, beside one of his assistants.

Jordan was talking on his cell phone. When he got off, he looked particularly grim. His glance spotted Sara immediately. "That was Heumann," he said. "There's been another development outside."

TO JORDAN, "another development" was a euphemism for yet another gruesome discovery.

"What is it?" Sara asked as she walked beside him down the apartment hallway.

"Possibly evidence in another murder," he barked. At her sudden intake of breath, he said more gently, "That's not certain yet, though."

"What—" she began again, but then they reached the outer door and Jordan ushered her through it.

"Stick close by me," he commanded, then added, "Please." He glanced over at her, to find that she had managed to shoot him a small, amused smile. Despite his grim mood, he found himself returning it.

Oh, Sara, he thought. *If only I could protect you from all this.*

As if she would let him.

He spotted the crowd of law enforcement personnel right away. They stood behind the yellow crime scene tape but near the street, beside the medical examiner's wagon. Artificial lights still illuminated the area. "Over there," Jordan told Sara.

He saw right away that the female uniformed officer who was Sara's too-talkative friend, June Roehmer, was crying. Her partner, Ramon Susa, looked angry and helpless at the same time.

But there had been no reason to remove either from Jordan's suspect list. One of them could be a darned good actor.

He wanted to take June by the shoulders and shake

her, get her to divulge who she had spoken with about Sara. He would, in fact, quiz her a little later, when he had the time. But he doubted that the information would help. Anyone she'd told could have spoken with a dozen more people, and they, in turn, could have passed the news along.

Near them, Carroll Heumann was talking with Lloyd Pederzani and Dwayne Gould. They all seemed to be looking at something that Pederzani held in his hand.

"Why don't you see if you can help June?" Jordan told Sara. He didn't want her to actually see what the others were examining—if it was as Heumann had described on the phone.

"Why?" she asked suspiciously.

"Because I think it would be better for you."

"And I think I would be better off staying with you, Jordan."

"Remaining in the thick of things?" He tried to act angry, but admired her persistence nonetheless.

"You've got it," she replied.

SARA REALIZED Jordan was just trying to protect her—but she wanted to know what he thought she needed protection *from*. When he approached Heumann and the others, Sara followed.

But Jordan wasn't the only one trying to protect her. Lloyd Pederzani stepped away from the group and came toward her. Worry seemed to make the medical examiner's lean face all the more gaunt. He wore a white shirt that did nothing to hide his thinness. "Hi, Sara. Why don't you and I go somewhere to talk?"

Uneasiness prickled along Sara's back. "Why?" Her voice was small and hoarse. Lloyd had been a friend of her father's, he had told her so, and she thought she recalled something now about their closeness.

"A piece of evidence has been found here." He stopped and looked helplessly toward Jordan, who had reached Heumann's side and taken an item into his hand.

"What is it?" Sara felt certain, from everyone's reaction, that she didn't want to know. And that made her realize she *needed* to know.

"Sara—" The kind, sad-looking older man touched her shoulder. "Leave it alone. It'll be better that way."

"You may be right." She tried to smile at the medical examiner, then gave up the effort.

In the meantime, June and Ramon had become part of the group that was discussing…whatever it was that remained in Jordan's hand. June still appeared overwrought, Ramon angry.

Sara approached Jordan, trying to discern what it was that he held. It looked like a small jar.

In a moment, she, too, had joined the group. Lloyd remained at her side. Carroll Heumann seemed even more agitated than normal as he demanded of Jordan, "Turn it over to Pederzani. Let him figure out if that's what it really is, or if it's some kind of miserable joke."

"I can take it back with me," Dwayne Gould suggested. "I'll be going to the lab soon as the victim is released."

"Just get it out of here," sobbed June. Her partner Ramon patted her gently on the shoulder.

Curiosity—possibly morbid curiosity—shoved Sara into the middle of the group. Without asking Jordan's permission, she gently took the jar from him.

"Sara, no," he said. But she held it up so she could look into it.

Something bobbed around inside—a long, white object in liquid. Sara couldn't quite make it out. She turned the jar until she saw a label. She read it. "Stu Shepard—little finger."

Sara felt herself blanch, but she made herself look at the object again. Surely it wasn't really that...but she couldn't tell....

She heard something then. Something low and familiar—a soft jingling. She had heard it before. And it signified death....

"Oh, no—" she heard herself say, as if from a distance. Someone took the jar from her, she wasn't certain who. She felt an arm go around her shoulder, supporting her.

"It'll be okay, Sara," said Jordan. He sounded as if he spoke from far away, the other end of a long tunnel.

Before she could respond, a horrible thunder resounded through her ears, pounding into her head, as something a block from where they stood exploded in a ball of fire.

Chapter Twelve

"Come with me, Sara." Jordan's voice somehow penetrated the haze that was Sara's mind. "I can't leave you here."

"All right," she agreed. But as she tried to follow she realized her legs had turned to soft tofu.

The others from their group ran toward the blaze that lit up the night sky. Even June, Ramon at her side, headed in the direction of the blast. They were followed by Carroll Heumann, who managed to move relatively quickly despite his bulk, as well as lanky Lloyd Pederzani, and the older and slower Dwayne Gould. Some of the uniformed police officers who had been milling around the area hurried ahead. Others remained at the murder site, on Heumann's orders, to keep that area secure.

It appeared to Sara that a car had erupted into an inferno. Screams filled the air and a siren blared in the distance.

Sara tried to keep up with Jordan's fast pace, but she stumbled. He grabbed her with his strong hands and kept her from falling. She appreciated it. She appreciated *him*.

But she knew he wanted to be where the action was. Where he was needed. And she was holding him back.

"Go on ahead, Jordan," she said.

But he stayed by her side.

In a few minutes they neared the area of the blast. Some uniformed officers from the other crime scene had already established a police line and were working to keep civilians back. A couple used foam extinguishers on the car. Others were stringing yellow crime scene tape.

"Any idea what happened?" Jordan called to the nearest cop.

"Couple of witnesses said the thing just exploded. No one inside, fortunately."

In a few minutes the fire department arrived. The remaining flames were quickly extinguished as the members of the police department watched. What had once been a sedan of indeterminate color had become a mass of scorched, twisted metal and ash sitting just beyond the reach of a streetlight's illumination. The odors of charred paint and scorched metal and burned fuel filled the air.

"What caused it?" Jordan asked.

"There's a lot of gasoline around here," one of the firemen said, hosing down a dark, oozing puddle on the road. "Too much. I'd suggest that some of you police types investigate. Looks like arson to me—probably set off by an incendiary device with a timer."

As Sara watched, still in her own haze, Jordan turned to Carroll Heumann—just as the acting police chief's cell phone rang. "It what?" he demanded into the phone. "What do you mean?" He listened for a moment, then declared, "I'll be there in a minute. And you'd better have found it by then."

"What's happened?" Jordan asked.

"The murder weapon—that damned steak knife—has suddenly gone missing."

"That can't be!" Lloyd Pederzani exclaimed. "I expressly told my technician to keep hold of it."

"Well, your technician fouled up," Heumann growled. "That was Ben Marvin. He's still in the apartment gathering evidence in the murder, and he said the knife's disappeared."

"We'll see about that," Lloyd said.

The group split up in a hurry. Some quickly retraced their steps back to the apartment building. There was still plenty of illumination along the street from overhead lights. Others stayed around the fire. Sara barely kept track of who was where. She just stayed with Jordan.

"Shouldn't we go back to the murder scene?" Sara knew her question lacked enthusiasm, but she doubted she could work up excitement about anything just then.

Too much was happening.

"Probably," Jordan said, "but something's going on here I don't understand. We were lured here for a reason, and I intend to find out why."

"Who has possession of the…that glass jar now?" Sara felt sick thinking about it. Surely it didn't really contain her brother's finger—did it?

"I do," Jordan said. He patted a bulge in the side pocket of his trousers. "I didn't want to trust it to— Hey!"

Sara looked in the direction Jordan was facing. A young man on a bicycle rode by—and as he passed through the glow from the streetlight she could see that he was waving a gasoline can in the air and laughing.

"That's no coincidence, Sara. That kid is trying to

lure me away, and I want to find out who put him up to it. I'm going to catch him.''

"Let's go," she said, then hesitated. "No, you go ahead. I'll only slow you down.''

He looked ready to argue.

"Go," she repeated. "You're wasting time.''

He nodded reluctantly, looking around. "All right. But you stay close to the firefighters. You should be safe here. I'll be back before they've got this mess mopped up. Okay?''

"Okay," Sara said. He searched her expression for sincerity. "Get going," she insisted. "I'll become best friends with the firemen. Really.''

He must have accepted her word, for in a moment she watched his large but graceful form sprint after the bicyclist. The kid was weaving around in the sparse nighttime traffic, turning back now and then to taunt the man he obviously knew followed him.

No, it was no coincidence. What was happening here?

Jordan would figure it out. With Sara's help, of course—as soon as her mind began functioning again.

She watched as the last of the fire was extinguished, heard the sizzling of water on flame.

It wasn't just her memory that was acting strange now. Her entire mind seemed to have gone peculiar. She felt out of sync with everything going on around her.

And in her thoughts, she kept hearing the jingling of keys.

Just as she had back by the murder scene.

Just as she had…when? It would come to her. It had to.

In the meantime she would do as she'd promised. She would stay right here, where there were lots of lights and plenty of people around. Big, husky firemen who, though they weren't looking after her, surely wouldn't allow anyone to harm her.

She would wait for Jordan to return. Jordan. Her husband—no matter how unwilling he was. The man she had, despite all her better judgment, begun to love.

She had promised him she'd stay, and she had meant it.

Until she saw an unfamiliar young man in jeans and a T-shirt, with a diamond stud in his ear walk by— waving a plastic bag at her. Inside, in the illumination from the street lamp, she could see that it was a steak knife. Its tip was moist and red.

Someone had intentionally lured Jordan away. Now it was her turn. She shouldn't go. She had promised.

But if she stayed here, the guy with the missing murder weapon would get away.

She might not be able to apprehend him, but she could at least keep an eye on him.

He was heading back in the direction of the scene of the murder. There was a lot of light along the way, and there would be plenty of backup there. And Sara would be careful.

As a dispatcher, she didn't wear a Sam Browne, the heavy belt on which uniformed officers carried a lot of equipment. She didn't have a gun or baton, or even a radio.

She couldn't call in her position, or what she was doing.

Nevertheless, she began to follow.

JORDAN CAUGHT THE KID on the bicycle a block away. It wasn't that his own speed was so extraordinary, or that the bicyclist had any trouble.

No, the kid, who was probably only twelve years old, stopped under a streetlight at a corner and waited for him. "Are you Jordan Dawes?" he asked.

Jordan wasn't surprised the kid knew his name. He'd been certain this was part of the setup. He just didn't know why. Still, he prepared to pull his gun from his shoulder holster as he approached. Even youngsters could be dangerous. "That's me," he answered.

"I was told to give you this." The kid, thin and gangly in adolescence, held out the gas can. "Some guy gave me ten bucks."

"Can you describe him?" Jordan flashed his badge. "Santa Gregoria Police," he said, just in case the kid didn't get it.

The kid *did* get it. His eyes bugged, and he looked suddenly frightened. "I d-didn't see him," he stammered. "He called to me from inside that big ambulance near the apartment building down the street, where all the cops were."

"The medical examiner's wagon?"

"Yeah," the kid said. "He told me what he wanted me to do. Said the car would explode, then I was supposed to...hey, you don't think the guy blew up the car, do you?" The boy looked even more terrified.

Jordan said, "Someone poured gasoline on it." He nodded toward the plastic container the boy still held. "And the only one I see with any is you."

"I didn't do it, mister. Really." His voice shook.

"No, I don't believe you did. What did the guy look like?"

The kid shrugged. "Don't know. It was dark and he stayed in the van."

Jordan sighed. "You come back with me right now so we can have a little talk." Jordan made sure that the kid on the bike followed him back toward the burned car, though he doubted he'd learn anything of use from him.

But he didn't want to be away from Sara any longer. At least she would be there, surrounded by the firemen. She had promised.

But he should have known better. When he got back to the hulk of the car, Sara was nowhere near the car.

Jordan slammed his hand against a nearby light post. Dammit, why couldn't the woman listen, just this once? Hadn't she realized it was all a setup? He'd warned her.

Whoever had lured him away from her had also lured her away from safety.

"You okay, Mr. Dawes?" the boy on the bicycle asked.

"Tell me again how someone paid you—" And then it dawned on Jordan. The boy had said something about the medical examiner's wagon.

Dwayne Gould had driven it here to collect the latest body.

Gould had been part of the Santa Gregoria law enforcement team for years.

He had known Stu Shepard. From what Jordan recalled, there'd even been mention that Stu had once accused Gould of carelessness in transporting a decedent from a crime scene—an accident had resulted that muddled the determination of cause of death so that a perpetrator walked free. Maybe it hadn't been accidental—perhaps Gould had even been the murderer that time.

As he probably had been before…and after. Many times.

Being with the medical examiner's office, he might even have had access to Stu's body, after his murder—if that finger in the jar Jordan still had was actually Stu's.

He had been high all along on Jordan's suspect list.

And Jordan had fallen for Gould's distraction.

But he was all but certain now that he knew his perpetrator. He would find Sara, before it was too late.

He had to.

And then he would take care of Gould.

He reached the outside of the apartment building… but the medical examiner's wagon was just pulling away.

Just in case, Jordan used his cell phone to call Ben Marvin. The criminologist was just finishing up his work inside the murder scene.

And he hadn't seen Sara since she'd left with Jordan.

SARA'S HEAD HURT.

She opened her eyes nevertheless—to see only darkness.

But she was moving. She realized then she was in some kind of vehicle. She lay on the floor, her hands tied. Her legs, too.

She moaned.

What had happened to her?

She had been with Jordan. A car had exploded, and he had chased after a kid with a can of gasoline.

She was to stay. She did stay.

And then—the person with the plastic bag and knife!

She had, of course, figured it could be a trap. But she had fully intended to be cautious, to stay far away from her subject, to simply watch where he was heading.

It had helped that they were heading back toward the murder scene, where there would be backup for her.

In fact, she had nearly reached the building when... when...

Something had struck her from behind. She had flailed out and touched—some kind of vehicle. She was on the wrong side of the building. The crowd had dispersed, probably followed the explosion. No one could see her, and she had fallen....

And here she was.

Oh, Jordan, her mind cried out. *I'm sorry.*

She hadn't listened to him. And now the person who'd killed her brother and father had her, too.

She knew Jordan had wanted vengeance for her brother. And he had felt terribly guilty that her father had been killed on his watch, and she'd been injured.

He would feel guiltier still when she died.

It's not your fault, she thought fiercely. *It was my own carelessness.* But she doubted it would matter to him.

The vehicle slowed. Could she find a way to get out? But then it speeded up again; they were going around a curve.

At least she was awake now. Maybe she could take her captor by surprise.

But how could she use self-defense techniques while trussed like a turkey?

She'd find a way. She had to.

She lay quietly for a while, trying to figure out by sounds and motions where she was. But she had no idea.

And then the vehicle stopped.

The engine was shut off.

Sara held her breath. Was this the end?

She waited, every muscle within her on the alert. She would find a way to survive—and not just for her own sake. For Jordan's peace of mind, as well.

A door opened—the rear door. She was in some kind of a van. Light flooded inside. She tensed, waiting.

And then there were sounds of a struggle. "Hey!" cried a voice. "What are you doing?" There was a noise like fist on bone, then silence.

A backlit figure appeared in the doorway. By then, Sara had been able to see enough to figure out that she was in the medical examiner's ambulance—and that, strapped onto a gurney near her was the bagged body from the apartment. She tensed.

The figure climbed into the compartment with her—and it was then that she moved. She kicked out, her feet colliding with flesh. There was an incoherent yell—a man's. Good. She had aimed where a blow would do her the most good against a male.

And then a voice—beloved despite its agony, said, "Dammit, Sara, settle down and let me rescue you."

JORDAN HELPED SARA from the ambulance. They were in downtown Santa Gregoria, outside the municipal building, in its well-lighted parking lot.

"I'm really sorry," she told him.

Jordan's face was pale, but he managed a lopsided grin at her. "So am I."

He cut away the rope, and she massaged her bruised and bleeding wrists, but only for a moment. Then she reached over to touch the rough cheek of the man who was so gently rubbing her ankles where the ropes had caused even further bruising.

"How did you find me?"

He related the story of what the bicyclist had told him, then asked, "Would it do me any good to inquire why you decided to leave the firemen and go off on your own?"

"It might." She told about the young man brandishing what had appeared to be the murder weapon. "Since he headed back toward the murder site, I thought there would be plenty of backup, and I didn't intend to get near the kid anyhow. I hadn't figured on everyone's having left. That kid was probably paid off like your bicyclist, and he got away." And then she hesitated. "Who was the killer, Jordan?"

A groan sounded from outside the ambulance. "See for yourself."

Sara was barely able to put weight on her legs, but she managed to stay upright as she looked down at the man Jordan had just caught. His hands were cuffed behind his back.

How had grizzled old Dwayne Gould caused such havoc in her life?

"I DIDN'T DO IT," Dwayne cried.

They were inside the police station, in a small, dreary holding room with musty concrete walls. Jordan was watching, and not participating, as Carroll Heumann interrogated the older man.

After all, Jordan's role here in Santa Gregoria was over. They had caught the man who'd killed Stu and Casper.

Who'd hurt Sara, and not just once.

His Sara. His beautiful, brave—and sometimes fool-hardy wife.

Oh, yes. It was much better if someone else conducted the interrogation. This way, Jordan could stay back and work hard on controlling his temper.

Too bad the killer hadn't been Carroll Heumann. There was still something about the guy that Jordan didn't like. Something shady and surreptitious and reptilian.

But not, apparently, murderous.

"Of course you didn't do it," Heumann said to Gould, who sat on a chair facing his interrogators. "And Mrs. Dawes just happened to tie herself up, hit herself on the head and throw herself in the back of your ambulance."

"No, no, that's not what I'm trying to say. I must have driven her from the crime scene, but I didn't know it. I didn't put her in there. Someone else must have."

They had read Dwayne his Miranda rights, and so far he had waived his right to an attorney. They'd gotten everything on videotape. There could be no slip-ups.

This son of a gun was going to be tried for multiple murders. When he was found guilty...well, he could rot in prison or die for his crimes; Jordan didn't care, as long as he paid.

"And just who, Mr. Gould, do you suggest did the evil deed of hurting Mrs. Dawes and tossing her in your vehicle?"

"I don't know," wailed the older man.

He put on a good act, Jordan thought. But he hardly expected the man to confess even to this one crime, let alone all the related murders—at least not at first.

But now that they had their perpetrator in custody, all the evidence in each of the serial killings—slim though it was—could be sifted again to make a case against Gould.

And Jordan was certain it would, in each instance, be a good case.

After all, Gould had been in Santa Gregoria law enforcement, more or less, as Stu had suggested. He had fought with Stu. He had been an invited guest at Jordan's wedding to Sara—so he had had plenty of opportunity to slip away and kill Casper, who had suddenly been closing in on him.

And to hurt his sweet, headstrong Sara, who had been in the way.

Gould had been part of the law enforcement team, transporting bodies from place to place. He probably got a kick out of that. An even bigger kick out of fooling everyone.

How had he kept all the blood from the gory crimes he committed from getting all over him?

They would find out, as questioning continued.

Jordan was certain they had their ''Executioner.''

Wasn't he?

''IT'S ALL OVER, then?'' Sara yawned and looked over at Jordan. They were in his white Mustang, and he was driving.

He looked even more exhausted than she felt. But even so, he was the most devastatingly handsome man she had ever met.

Or so she still believed—even without the rest of her memory. Not even the latest blow on the head had jarred it back completely.

''It looks that way, though we still have some investigating to do to tie Dwayne to all the killings. We've gotten a warrant, and a team is already at his apartment looking for evidence. We don't want to delay in finding everything we can to tie him to what went on last night—the latest murder, the car explosion, hiring those two kids to distract you and me.''

"Did Dwayne admit any of it?"

"He denied everything, but I hardly expected otherwise. An admission on even something small could lead to a trail to the murders.''

It was early morning, but they were on their way home. Sara had waited at the station while he helped in the interrogation. She hadn't wanted to sleep anyway. Nor had she wanted to go home alone. Even though she would no longer be in danger.

Not if the killer had actually been caught.

Sara wasn't entirely convinced it was Dwayne, though everyone else seemed to think so. His own actions certainly pointed to him.

But without recalling the night of her father's murder, how would Sara know? She had nothing to base her doubts on, any more than she would have anything to base a certainty on.

And…maybe she simply wasn't convinced because she didn't want to be. If the case was solved, there was no reason for Jordan to stay here.

To stay married to her.

A pang of desolation shot through her. She must have moved, since Jordan glanced over at her. They had halted at a traffic light, several blocks from their house. Jordan had insisted that they make a stop at the hospital to have her head checked again, after the latest blow. A new CAT scan and a couple of hours later, they'd been sent on their way.

"Are you all right?" he asked.

"Just tired."

"Since your head is okay, you can sleep as long as

you want now. You won't have anything more to worry about.''

He reached over and took her hand in his firm grip. His flesh was cool from gripping the steering wheel, but still managed to be utterly comforting.

Temporarily, she told herself.

Their marriage was nearly over.

She sighed out loud.

''That didn't sound like a relieved sigh to me,'' he said dryly.

''It was intended to show my utter happiness,'' she contradicted with a smile.

''I'd hate to hear one of your sighs of misery, then.''

Sara managed to laugh as they pulled into the driveway. They were home. Together.

How many more times would that happen?

When they got inside, Jordan headed straight for the kitchen. Sara followed and sank onto one of the wooden chairs. She wanted to go to bed—but even more, she wanted to stay in Jordan's presence.

It was a luxury she would soon miss.

Jordan remained by the door. ''So,'' he said, ''are you going to make breakfast or am I?''

''You're hungry?'' Sara felt as if a lump of ashes from the car that had exploded had settled into her stomach. Food was the furthest thing from her mind. She stared at a half-filled napkin holder on the table, idly considering that she would have to add some napkins soon.

''Solving a case always stimulates my appetite. How about yours?'' There was a strange note in his voice.

Sara replied, ''I don't remem…'' Her voice trailed off as she looked over at him. He wasn't raiding the pantry or the refrigerator. He was staring at her. His deep, deep blue eyes held a look of longing and lust that made her stop breathing. The morning light streaming in through the windows formed shadows in the rugged hollows of Jordan's cheeks and illuminated the shadow of beard that had grown since he had last shaved.

Their gazes held for a long moment. "Sara." His voice caressed her name at the same time it imbued it with a hint of question.

That lump moved up into her throat…at the same time she felt a heated dampness begin in the vicinity of her thighs. She understood his inquiry without it being further vocalized—and knew the answer she wanted to give.

She stood and approached him. He didn't move.

She ran one hand beneath his leather vest, up the outside of his shirt. She noticed that he had already put away his gun, for he no longer wore his holster. His body heat had warmed his clothing. She felt his muscles bunch, though he otherwise remained still.

"Do I have to do all the work?" she whispered, her head tilted back so she could watch the fire blaze in his eyes.

"Not all of it," he whispered.

Ever so slowly, he bent toward her. She trembled in anticipation, even as she continued to run her fingers over the hard planes of his chest, memorizing his masculine form from outside his shirt. And then his mouth found hers.

The kiss captivated Sara's every sense. She heard Jordan's breathing grow ragged, her own small moans of need. His arms wrapped around her, pulling her so close that she felt the fit of the hard contours of his chest against her sensitive breasts, the bulge within his trousers that pressed against her stomach. His lips were firm on hers, and as her mouth opened she tasted the heated spiciness of his tongue. The shadow of his beard scratched deliciously at the skin of her cheeks. She inhaled his incomparable masculine scent. Though her eyes were closed, she saw his look of lust and need, for she had already memorized it.

He pulled back slightly. "Sara," he whispered hoarsely once more. "I don't—"

She opened her eyes, pressed her fingers to his lips, saw the concern in his desire-filled eyes. "I know."

She didn't want to hear what he would say, for if he gave warnings of no promises, no future, he would ruin the moment. She knew the truth already.

"Please, Jordan," she murmured. "Let's go upstairs."

Chapter Thirteen

Sara had never made love with a man in her bedroom in this house before. She was certain of it as she stood in the doorway with Jordan, looking at the queen-size bed that dominated the room…and called them to it.

She had been married previously. Though she still could not recall anything about it, Jordan had told her so.

And yet she was sure she had not brought her husband here, to her childhood bedroom of burgundies and blues—the man who had hurt her so much that she had been willing to marry again for reasons far removed from love. As if she had no longer believed in love.

Before.

They stepped inside the room, and it was as if they had awaited that instant forever. Sara turned toward Jordan and tugged off his vest. He moved willingly to assist her. She began to undo the buttons of his shirt…as he did the same with her uniform.

"Faster, Jordan," she commanded with a hazy smile on her face.

"Your wish is my command." It seemed mere moments before the rest of her clothing puddled at her feet on the floor. Sacrilegious, she thought, for her uniform to be treated like that—but she didn't want to take the time to hang it up.

Not now, while she was trying to meet Jordan's speed. Her hands shook as she pulled off his shirt and undershirt, then reached for the button on his jeans.

She couldn't avoid touching the area that bulged so deliciously in front—as if she wanted to avoid it. "Oh, Sara." Jordan stilled her hand right there as though he would explode if she moved it.

She would explode if she *didn't* move it, but for a moment she simply reveled in the feel of him throbbing beneath her fingers. Then she tried hard to be judicious in her touch as she pulled down his zipper. She stripped away his jeans and boxers all in one fluid motion that caused her to bend so that her eyes were on a level with that marvelous male member that had caused Jordan's consternation. Now, it engendered Sara's admiration. And sparked a sensuality inside her that she didn't even know she had.

He took her hand. Together, they managed to make it to the bed. Jordan pulled Sara down beside him. His hands stroked first one breast, then the other. The sensation made Sara nearly scream. She felt virginal, as if the experience of having a man's touch on her naked body was brand new. She knew it wasn't. She had once been married. She had undoubtedly experienced sex before.

Still, as far as she could remember, she had never previously felt this incredible arousal.

Jordan replaced his hands on her breasts with his lips, taking her nipples one by one into his mouth and sucking gently.

"Please, Jordan," Sara begged, not entirely certain what she was asking, except that she wanted more.

And she wanted to touch him more, as well. She explored his bare chest, with all of its muscular bulges, then moved so that she could reach around to the firm hills of his buttocks. That pressed them more closely together, and she could feel his erection hard and hot against her. It was his turn to plead, even as he reached between her thighs and stroked her, inside and out, with his fingers. "Now, Sara?"

"Oh, yes," she breathed.

And then he was inside her. It was a deliriously sensuous feeling just to have his hardness filling her. When he started to move, she gasped, then reveled in the rhythm, moving her hips to meet him as he plunged, then pulled back in a starburst of sensuality that drove and drove and finally spilled Sara over the edge of infinite sensation.

Afterward, she cuddled close to him, her exhaustion total now in spent pleasure. His arms were around her as his breathing finally slowed. She rested her head on his shoulder, feeling sleep finally ready to overcome her.

She felt complete.

Hadn't she once thought the moon would sink screaming into the Pacific before she made love with Jordan? If she held her breath now, she just might be able to hear that wondrous distant cry.

"Are you okay?" Jordan's voice seemed to come from a distance, as if he, too, were falling asleep.

"Mm-hmm," she murmured affirmatively. "Couldn't be better."

Which wasn't entirely true.

She could have been much better if she knew that this was not a one-morning stand with the man who was her husband. If she dared to hope for more mornings, afternoons and even long, lustful nights with him.

If there might be a marriage of more than police procedure—one not destined to disintegrate as soon as their job was done.

But she couldn't tell him that. Not now, especially. She didn't want to spoil the moment by causing him to recoil from her wishes as he tried to explain once more why he had come, why he was leaving.

His chest began to rise and fall rhythmically. Sara knew that Jordan was asleep.

As tired as she was, she remained awake, still curled close to him, for a long time.

HE HADN'T PLANNED on making love with Sara, Jordan thought later that morning when he woke up beside her, beneath the rumpled burgundy sheets on her bed. In fact, he had planned *against* it.

But he had certainly fantasized—constantly—about giving in to the passion he felt every time he looked at her. And the incredibly erotic reality had been even more delightful than his most stimulating fantasies had been.

Light filtered in through the miniblinds at the windows. Sara's back was to him now, and her adorable butt rested against his front. Only he wasn't resting; not now. All of the blood in his body seemed to be rushing to one, growing area....

"Well, good morning!" Sara wiggled her behind against him, and he groaned.

He brushed some of her sleep-tossed dark hair away from her ear and growled into it, "Don't do that unless you mean business."

She shivered slightly, and he rubbed his hand against

her arm. His voice had given her goose bumps, and he smiled. "I always mean business," she murmured, still without turning toward him. "Or at least I think so, if I could recall—"

He pulled her toward him, moving her quickly so that they were face-to-face. He smothered what he assumed would be a dissertation on her memory loss by a deep, searching kiss. Or maybe it had been an attempt to distract him. If it was the latter, it definitely failed.

In short order, Sara seemed as ready as he was to continue their highly sensual activities.

Much later, he watched her as her lovely hazel eyes came back into post-passion focus and her breathing slowed. Tenderly, he pushed strands of dampened hair away from her face. Her smooth cheeks were flushed— and he had never seen anyone more beautiful.

"Thank you, Sara," he whispered.

Her full lips curved upward almost impishly. "For what?"

"For...this. For you. For this morning."

"And are you going to thank me every morning?" Her tone was teasing, but there was a wariness in her beautiful hazel eyes.

He sighed, gripping her arm with his hand and letting his thumb push gentle patterns into her soft flesh. "Sara, if what you're asking is if I'll stay, you know the answer. You knew it before."

"Of course. And I understand that nothing has changed." She still kept her tone light, but he could hear pain behind her words. She no longer met his gaze.

"Sara, I didn't mean to hurt you. I got carried away earlier. We both did. All along I've kept my hands off you—" He felt her arm stir beneath his grasp and amended, "Almost. This whole idea of your father's was well meant, but in many ways it caused more harm than good."

She turned her back on him, but this time her bare flesh did not rest against his. "The serial killer has been caught."

"The cost was high. More deaths, including your father's."

"And my memory loss, though it's not as irrevocable."

"Yes, that's a cost, too. Sara—"

Once again she faced him. This time she held the sheets so that hardly any skin beneath her neck was exposed. "Don't," she commanded.

"Don't what?"

"Weren't you going to tell me again the terms of our bargain—yours and mine and Dad's? How we all decided we'd work together to catch Stu's killer, and how you and I would get married, but only temporarily. That worked for you, since you were a dedicated officer of the peace and Stu had been one of your closest friends. You didn't understand how Stu had been taken by surprise and killed. In the SEALs, he'd seemed as much of a by-the-book, alert military man as your father had taught you. You weren't dating anyone, at least not seriously, so you came, but always with the intention of returning to your beloved Texas Rangers."

Jordan looked at her in amazement. "Sara, I didn't tell you all that."

"And then there was *my* rationale," she continued. She sat up, still clutching the sheet so her tug on it almost bared him below his chest. He didn't care, unless it would embarrass her; she had seen everything before anyway. "I'd been married before to a man who'd left me for a job in a larger town. I'd expected to join him when he settled in, but not when I realized his settling had been with another woman.'' She paused. Tears flowed down her soft cheeks. Her eyes had reddened, but were no less beautiful. "His name was Ricky."

"Sara, I didn't tell you that, either. You must have remembered."

"Yes," she said softly. "I remember my mother's passing away now. I remember Stu, too, and how much it hurt to lose him. And my dad—oh, how it still hurts." She swallowed a sob. When Jordan made a move as though to come closer to her in comfort, she looked away. "And I also remember why I married you."

"Why is that?"

"Because I wouldn't have to get close to you. It wouldn't hurt to lose you, since it would be over very soon."

With that, she pulled the sheet off the bed and him, wrapped it the rest of the way around herself, and hurried into the bathroom.

SARA'S SHIFT that day didn't start until early afternoon. She told Jordan to go on to the station without her. After all, with the killer caught, she was perfectly safe.

And she wanted to be alone.

She sat at the kitchen table, forcing herself to concentrate on her breakfast of orange juice and a bagel.

"Maybe I should add some gingko biloba," she said. The stuff was reputed to be good for the memory.

Her memory *was* returning, but too slowly, and still in small pieces. She shivered, as she now remembered Stu and his murder, and the horror of that time.

She remembered her father, too, and how dear he had been. She still didn't recall, though, the attack on her that had damaged her head...and her ability to recollect.

Nor did she remember her father's murder.

She did, however, remember all about that horrible excuse for a deserting husband, Ricky.

Worst of all, she remembered those days years ago when she had been an awkward teenager, and Stu had brought Jordan home during their basic training in the navy.

It was then that she had fallen in love with Jordan.

Of course it had been a teenage crush. But it had never completely gone away, and she had seen Jordan, now and then over the years, when he had come to visit Stu. He had only grown more special with age. But of course he had always gone away and left her. He had never been hers in the first place.

Initially when she had married, it had been because she'd known she would never attract Jordan, or find anyone else as kind and brave and handsome. She had settled for second—or maybe ten millionth—best: Ricky.

She had honestly fooled herself into thinking she was through with all men before she'd agreed to marry Jordan. That she was invulnerable to deeper feelings.

She would never have intentionally subjected herself to the heartache she now experienced. Her youthful crush had turned into full-blown, hurtful, hateful, unrequited love...for her husband.

Her *temporary* husband, with whom she had just made the most memorable love.

Why hadn't those memories just stayed hidden?

She chugged the rest of her orange juice and refrigerated the remaining three-quarters of her bagel. "Okay, Sara Shepard," she told herself. "It's time to leave for work."

This time, when she left the "Dawes" off the end of her name, it was entirely intentional.

Then why did her name sound so suddenly stripped?

JORDAN ROSE STIFFLY from where he knelt on the floor in Dwayne Gould's small first-floor apartment. He had been spending a lot of time on his knees. He wanted to set an example for the relatively inexperienced criminologist Ben Marvin and for the crime scene technicians he had helped to train. He also wanted to make sure they hadn't missed anything.

Though there had been other searches of more horrific crime scenes since his arrival, this place could be the most important of all.

It could link Dwayne Gould to each of the murders.

This time, as Jordan rose, he clutched a pair of tweezers in his fingers. The tweezers held a used latex glove that he had found beneath the sofa. There were dark stains on it. Blood.

And Jordan was certain that it would match the blood of one of the murder victims.

Might it be Casper's? It was unlikely to be old enough to be Stu's.

Before Jordan left, he at least had to give closure to Sara on the murders of her family members.

Before he left... Why didn't that make him feel a rush of pleasure? He'd be going back to the life he loved.

But without the woman he lo—

"Jordan? Are you ready to bag that?"

Ben Marvin held out a plastic bag in which the glove would be stored until it could be examined further.

"Of course." Jordan used the tweezers to insert the glove into the bag.

Ben labeled the evidence for him. "We've found a whole package of surgical gowns in the other room," he said. "More gloves, too." The young criminologist shook his prematurely graying head and grimaced. "Why would an ambulance driver need that stuff at home—unless he's also a murderer?"

Jordan nodded. "Looks as if we'll have plenty of evidence to convict Dwayne." And then he could leave with a clear conscience.

He recalled the thought interrupted by Ben—about Sara, and how he felt about her. And how it would feel to leave her.

He cared about her. A lot. It wasn't entirely due to the delights of sensual enjoyment that they had shared, though that hadn't hurt. Not at all.

In fact, it had felt mighty wonderful.

But she had remembered their pact. And in doing so, she made it absolutely clear that she had never intended their marriage to be permanent—and that she had not changed her mind.

Well, neither had he. And this wasn't the time to expend energy on that kind of brain—or heart—damage. He had work to complete.

He glanced around the apartment's combined living room-kitchenette. The guy had a collection of books on serial killers; his three-shelf book stand was full of them. Was he interested enough in them to have become one?

A couple of technicians slowly and methodically examined every square inch of the place, combing hair from the rug, even unscrewing the plates over electrical outlets to peer inside.

The stale odor of garlic and oregano in the air proclaimed Dwayne's love of Italian food. He was a surprisingly meticulous housekeeper. The only clutter was an array of brochures and magazines on retirement and travel.

Dwayne's personnel records showed him to be sixty-four years old—nearly ready for retirement. He apparently intended to enjoy his retirement by traveling—a nice, normal pastime for a man who, on the surface, appeared to be a nice, normal man.

Looks could be deceiving, Jordan thought. Had Dwayne intended to spread his serial murders to other towns?

"Hey, look at this!" The cry came from the bathroom. Jordan hurried in. Another of the technicians, himself wearing latex gloves, was extracting a green paper surgical gown from a plastic bag that was dripping wet. "It was inside the toilet tank." The gown, like the gloves, was bloodstained.

Once again, Jordan was certain it would match a victim's blood.

The evidence against Dwayne was becoming overwhelming.

Too overwhelming? Jordan couldn't help wondering—especially since the man had been so cautious at what had been left at the crime scenes.

Still, this was his home. He might have been brazen enough to assume it would never be searched, he would never be caught.

Or was it all a little too obvious?

"Looks like things here are going great." Carroll Heumann's bulk filled the bathroom door. "Some of the guys outside filled me in. Lots of thing stolen from the medical examiner's office that could have been used to cover his tracks. Lots of concealed evidence with blood on it.'' He rubbed his pudgy hands together as if in glee. "We've caught ourselves a killer. You looked in the freezer yet for body parts?''

"No," Jordan said, "I haven't.''

Neither he nor Ben had insisted yet on one of the technicians checking; if anything was there, it was likely to be grisly and he'd figured they might as well tackle that after making sure they had everything else. That way, if any technicians needed to be excused to toss their cookies, they wouldn't have to call anyone else in for additional help. In particularly ugly situations, that sometimes happened to even the most experienced investigator. Even Jordan had felt his stomach roll and jump now and then.

He hadn't gotten word yet on whether the finger in the jar had actually belonged to Stu Shepard. Jordan felt his mouth tighten in a grim line. If it was Stu's... He would be all the more inclined to make sure of the criminal's conviction. Dwayne had reputedly argued with Stu about botched evidence before his death.

Poor Sara—

"Excuse me, Carroll." Ben Marvin needed access to the small bathroom.

"Why don't we get out of the way here?" Jordan said. He motioned for Heumann to leave the room, and then he followed.

In the living room, Heumann's bulldog face took on an uncharacteristic grin, and he eased his bulk into the frayed, overstuffed couch beneath which the bloody glove had been hidden. "Glad it was one of Pederzani's folks who's guilty and not one of mine. You know the skinny little runt is after the police chief's job? He's campaigning, even though I'm a shoe-in.''

Heaven help poor Santa Gregoria if Heumann became the permanent chief, Jordan thought, though he kept it to himself. But mild Lloyd Pederzani instead? Would the medical examiner have the guts, let alone the knowledge, to run the police force?

He might be smart enough, but Jordan didn't know him well. He'd have to ask Sara her opinion.

He valued her opinion. Even without full memory, she had common sense.

What would his life be like back in Texas, when he didn't have her to ask? When he didn't have her to hold, to touch....

''So you going to support me or what, Dawes?'' Heumann was staring at him with narrowed eyes.

Jordan could hardly admit to him that he wouldn't be around to find out who became Casper Shepard's successor as police chief. As far as everyone here knew, his marriage to Sara was a love match, made in heaven and intended to last forever.

And until the murders were solved, the perpetrator convicted—

Dwayne Gould, Jordan told himself. It had to be Dwayne.

But weren't things here just a little too pat?

And wasn't Heumann just a little too cocky?

He'd said to look in the refrigerator. Did he know there would be something incriminating there?

''I've got evidence to gather now,'' Jordan said to Heumann, who still glowered at him for not immediately agreeing to support him. ''I'll worry about politics later. Tell you what. Ben's still busy in the bathroom with that bloody gown, and he's got most of his team in there, too. Why don't you and I look in the refrigerator?''

Heumann's face lit up. ''Sure. Why not? I always enjoy finding evidence against a killer, and judging by that damned finger you found, our boy likes body parts.''

''All of the bodies found were intact, weren't they?'' Jordan asked.

''Sure, but Dwayne works for the medical examiner. No problem for him to sever a digit here and there for fun before the body's released, right?''

''Right.'' Jordan didn't want to make a judgmental grimace. Instead, he headed for the refrigerator.

It was a small one, in keeping with the rest of the apartment. The lower compartment was for keeping foods cool; the upper was the freezer.

Jordan used his handkerchief to open the door; the technicians had already dusted the handle for fingerprints. He figured out right away that Dwayne had a penchant for imported beer and exotic cheeses. There was a small container of milk, a couple of suspect-looking eggs, and not much else.

And then they opened the freezer.

Dwayne also liked ice cream. Jordan removed the two half gallons in front...and learned something else that Dwayne must like: severed fingers.

There were two of them, in plastic bags, not jars this time.

Heumann jostled Jordan from behind, looking over his shoulder. He guffawed. ''See,'' he said. ''I told you. Pederzani's employee's a real nutcase.''

Chapter Fourteen

"I've just been to see Dwayne," Lloyd Pederzani told Sara. "The poor old fellow looks awful."

Lloyd didn't look so hot himself, Sara thought. The medical examiner had stopped to visit her at her dispatching station. He'd taken a seat beside her at the computer. She glanced toward him. His face was even more gaunt than usual—almost skeletal. A sadness quenched the usual twinkle in his eyes.

But Sara didn't hold the same sympathy for Dwayne that Lloyd appeared to have. "The 'poor old fellow' may be a murderer." She pushed the button to change the screen to a list of where all units were. Everything seemed in order, so she turned to face Lloyd. "Sorry if I sound insensitive, but—"

He reached over and patted her shoulder. "No, my dear. I'm the one who's insensitive. Poor—er, Dwayne is, after all, accused of killing your brother and father, among others. Do you… I mean…at the risk of sounding insensitive yet again, did you by any chance recall the attack on your father and you?"

"You mean, do I remember anything that might clear Dwayne?"

"Or convict him, if he deserves it."

Sara shook her head. "I am getting a little of my memory back, but not that, drat it all. But little by little, I seem to be improving. Meantime, I've every confidence in Jordan and his investigative abilities. He's got a great reputation in the Texas Rangers, or so he tells me. If he's finding evidence against Dwayne, then...."

She let her voice trail off. Lloyd looked so rueful that his face seemed to age before her eyes from middle-aged lines to elderly sag. But then he perked up. "Well, here's Jordan now. Maybe he'll have some news."

Sara didn't intend to perk up herself, just because Jordan had entered the room. After all, even though they'd spent a delightfully passionate morning together, it wouldn't happen again. He wasn't *really* her husband.

Well, maybe he *was* really her husband. But not for long.

"Hi, Sara," he said. "Lloyd."

"What's the news?" Lloyd asked eagerly. "You've searched Dwayne's apartment. You didn't find anything, did you?"

"Sorry, Lloyd." His deep blue eyes didn't look at the medical examiner as he described the condemning contents of Dwayne's apartment. Instead, they lit sympathetically on Sara's.

As he spoke, a few officers who'd been passing through the dispatch room stopped to listen. June and Ramon were among them.

"You've got him good, Jordan," Ramon said as Jordan paused.

"Could be," Jordan agreed.

Sara tried hard not to flinch, even when Jordan mentioned having found some rather gruesome evidence in the freezer. Though he wasn't explicit, she couldn't help but think of the jar containing a finger labeled as her brother's.

She bit her lower lip. Jordan was suddenly by her side. "I shouldn't have said anything, Sara. I'm sorry."

"I'm fine," she insisted. "And I'm glad to know. At least maybe we'll have closure soon." Closure that would result in Jordan's leaving. Though she had thought of little else all day, the reminder made her legs wobbly.

He apparently noticed and put a supporting arm around her shoulder. She gave him what she hoped was a neutral but gracious smile, then pulled gently away. She sat down at her computer, as though it had called to her, and pushed a few buttons. The screen indicated that one of the units was requesting a Code Seven—a meal break. She looked once more at the others' locations, then authorized it.

"So you really think it's Dwayne?" Lloyd sounded sorrowful, but Sara didn't glance at him again. She didn't like seeing sadness on such a kind man's face.

"It certainly looks that way," Jordan said.

BUT AS JORDAN had considered before, looks could be deceiving. After leaving Sara, Jordan had gone downstairs within the police headquarters to the small jail. Now, he was inside a secured visiting area with Dwayne.

"Then you knew nothing about the boxes of surgical gowns and latex gloves, the bloody glove under your sofa, the bloody gown in your toilet tank and the frozen body parts?" As he spoke, Jordan ticked each item off on his fingers.

Dwayne appeared old and frail. His face was pasty,

making even his silvery facial shadow stand out. Instead of his gray medical examiner's office outfit, he wore a bright blue jail uniform.

"I swear, sir. I didn't know about any of them. Someone must have planted them."

"Did you argue with Stu Shepard before he was murdered?"

"Well, yes, about some evidence, but that didn't mean I killed him."

Jordan stared hard into Dwayne's dull, wrinkle-shrouded eyes. "What about all those books you have on serial killers?"

He looked stricken. "You can't think that because I read about them, I actually do such things."

Jordan shrugged. "It doesn't matter what I think. It'll matter what a jury thinks. And all those books in your apartment, combined with all the other evidence—"

"The books are mine," Dwayne admitted. "But not the rest. Don't you see? I'm being framed."

Jordan kept his face blank, though a wry smile tugged at the corners of his lips. He had heard that before—many times. "And just who would do that?" he asked.

"The real murderer."

"Do you know who that is?"

The old man looked crestfallen. He studied his bony hands. "If I did, you can believe I'd tell you."

Yes, Jordan did believe that. And, strangely enough, he didn't disbelieve Dwayne Gould. Not that he totally accepted his protestations of innocence, but Jordan himself had thought things appeared too pat. Not that Dwayne was Albert Einstein incarnate, but he'd worked around law enforcement long enough to know not to keep bloody garments and body parts lying around his apartment as easily discoverable souvenirs, in case someone decided to pop in for a visit.

And if he were being framed?

That meant Jordan's job wasn't yet over. That he could stay here, pretending to be Sara's husband, for a while longer yet.

Was that one reason he was willing to consider Dwayne might be telling the truth?

Yes! But it wasn't the only one. His gut told him that he needed to do some more work—even if the outcome was simply to find more incontrovertible evidence against Dwayne.

He glanced at his watch. Sara's shift would not be over for another hour. That gave him time to go back upstairs and complete some paperwork before accompanying her home.

For if Dwayne were telling the truth, Sara could still be in danger.

THE EXECUTIONER wanted to laugh—except that it was premature.

Oh, yes, things were working just as planned. Dwayne Gould was the patsy, as The Executioner had devised. It had been simple to plant everything in the old man's apartment.

How helpful it was that dear Dwayne was so fascinated by serial killers. His collection of books on the subject would only help to convict him.

But was Jordan Dawes convinced? Hard to tell just what that damned intrusive Texas Ranger thought.

And from all The Executioner had heard, Sara seemed to be getting her memory back.

And so the next step would be just a bit tricky. Of

course The Executioner could handle it. The Executioner could handle anything. But instead of the usual, the next two deaths would need to appear accidental. Otherwise, all of the planning to frame Dwayne would be for naught.

With Jordan and Sara safely and carefully out of the way by apparent mishap, and not murder, no one else would question Dwayne's guilt for the other deaths. Not with the mounting evidence against him.

Poor Jordan and Sara. The newlyweds would not survive one more night of wedded bliss.

THE CALL came in on Jordan's cell phone while he was sitting at his desk, going over some of the evidence against Dwayne. Caller ID was blocked. "Dawes here."

"Detective?" The voice sounded strangled and faraway; there was a lot of static in the background. "You don't know me, but I was in the hotel at the time of your wedding. I saw something. I didn't want to get involved, but I read the papers. A lot of people are dying. I want to tell you what I saw."

"That's very nice of you. Give me your name, address and phone number, and I'll—"

"No. I want to remain anonymous."

Over the years Jordan had received plenty of similar calls. Sometimes they were from genuinely concerned citizens with helpful information. More often, they were from cranks who just wanted attention.

Occasionally, they were from the perpetrators themselves.

He was certain, suddenly, that that was the case. A hunch? Maybe. But he'd learned from long experience to go with his gut.

"How did you get my phone number?" Jordan asked, wanting to keep the person talking.

"It wasn't easy."

Jordan forced a laugh. "All right, then. How about if I meet you? You won't have to give me your name."

"I can tell you everything over the phone."

Sure, Jordan thought, *but since I think* you're *the murderer, I'd like to see you in person.* "Yes, you can do that," he said into the receiver, "but the problem is that with an anonymous phone call, with no return number, no recording, I won't be able to use what you say. If I meet you, record what you say but promise to play it back disguised electronically, then I'll be able to use it as evidence." That was an exaggeration, but it might get him an audience with his caller.

"Well…"

"Look, if you're serious about having information, tell me where and when to meet you. If you're not serious, then stop wasting my time." That was a little dangerous; he could lose the caller. On the other hand, it might rattle the person, get results.

Fortunately, that was what occurred. "All right. I live up in Gregoria Hills. I'll meet you in the parking lot behind the Santa G restaurant in half an hour."

"I'll be there," Jordan said.

ON THE WAY, Jordan considered his suspects, the motive, means and opportunity for each, the evidence. If he eliminated Dwayne, then—

Of course! There was really only one other person it could be.

He wouldn't call it in, though, till he could prove it. That should happen in a short while, if he handled things right. And there would still be enough time for him to get back and accompany Sara home.

He made it to the mountaintop restaurant in twenty minutes. He parked his borrowed, unmarked car behind the Santa G and activated the mobile computer. He typed in his ID number and his location, and transmitted the information to Sara. "Will contact if I need assistance."

He smiled as there was an immediate response on the screen. "What are you doing there? If you're on official business, do you have backup? Do you need backup? Why did you give me this information?"

"Because you're beautiful," he typed in. "And because I didn't want you to forget about me. Don't do anything now, but if you don't hear from me in half an hour, send backup."

He didn't give her time to respond. Ignoring the light rain, he cautiously got out of his car. He had come prepared. He was wearing a heavy jacket, and beneath it, bulletproof—and punctureproof—body armor. He already felt warm, though the special T-shirt he wore under his protective gear would help absorb perspiration.

Fully alert, he kept one hand poised at his side. His 9 mm Beretta was in its holster beneath his jacket.

"Hello?" he called, squinting into the foggy dimness behind the restaurant. He saw nothing other than the outlines of some cars, a garbage container.

He waited, listening, hearing nothing.

Until suddenly he heard the jingling of what sounded like keys. Behind him.

He whirled—to face just the person he suspected.

"Fancy seeing you here," Jordan said with a grim smile. He kept his tone placating—for the moment.

There would be plenty of time to tell the low-down murderer exactly what he thought—

Without a word, the person lunged at Jordan, one hand outstretched, the other hidden. The hidden hand came up quickly. Jordan, drawing his Beretta, just saw the needle as it was plunged into the side of his neck. "Hey!" he shouted—but it was too late to defend himself, too late to fire. The ground rushed up to meet him and the world went dark.

SARA WAS BESIDE herself. What was Jordan up to? As far as she knew, he was only working on solving the serial killings. The suspect was in jail.

Then why was he in an unmarked unit calling in his location to her?

While she had been communicating with him, an emergency call had come in, and she had had to send paramedics to a rest home.

When she tried to reach Jordan again, she received no answer. Not at first.

But then—a typed message came through. Something seemed strange about the transmission. Though it contained Jordan's ID number, it appeared to be from another unit. "Sara, are you still dispatching?"

"Yes. What's going on?"

"I have a surprise for you. Meet me at the Santa G restaurant up in Gregoria Hills."

A surprise for her? Maybe this was something he'd planned. She didn't remember birthdays—his or hers—or anniversaries, so if it was something like that, she had no idea.

Or maybe…could he be wanting to discuss their future?

Still, this was an odd way to do it. And he had left a message earlier that he might need backup.

"Do you need backup now?" she typed in.

"No," came the return message. "Everything's fine. See you soon."

But Sara wasn't so sure that everything was fine.

"Hi."

Sara turned to see Izzy Wilson behind her. "I'm glad you're here," she said to the dark-complected dispatcher whose shift was about to begin.

"Rough shift?"

"Sure was." Sara thought about telling Izzy about the evidence against Dwayne. Or had it already been on the news?

She showed her the computerized correspondence with Jordan. "I don't know what's going on, but I'm going to find out. I'll be there in twenty minutes. If you don't hear from either of us in half an hour, be sure to send backup, okay?"

"Okay—but maybe I should send someone now."

"No, Jordan said he didn't need any, but...well, this may just be a joke."

"Or something special." Izzy grinned. "You two are newlyweds, after all."

If you only knew the truth, Sara thought ruefully.

"Anyhow, it's drizzling outside. You be careful driving those steep mountain roads to that restaurant, you hear?"

"I hear you, Mom." Sara made herself laugh.

THE ROADS WERE SLICK. Night had begun to fall, and it was hard to see in the fog.

But, following the directions Izzy had given her, she

made it to the top of the mountain, and the restaurant, in just over twenty minutes.

She went inside the chalet-like restaurant and looked around. Izzy had told her it was the best place in Santa Gregoria for gourmet food. Not that Sara remembered that.

She didn't see Jordan in the dim, candlelit restaurant at any of the high-backed private booths or perfectly set tables, each complete with a vase with a single orchid.

She asked the formally clad maître d' if Jordan Dawes had been here, but he didn't know the name.

What was going on? Sara wondered. Jordan had asked her to come.

Sara returned to her car. Standing outside it, she used her cell phone to contact Izzy. "Has Jordan called? I don't see him here."

"No, ma'am. Do you want me to send backup?"

"Yes," Sara said.

But she wasn't going to wait, not if Jordan was in trouble.

Not that she'd be stupid about it. She got into her car. She would stay in it and drive around.

As she reached for the button to lock the doors, her door was suddenly pulled open. "Hey—!" she tried to call out, but something was stuffed into her mouth and she was pulled from the car. Frantically, she looked around. She was in a parking lot of a well-known restaurant. Surely someone would help.

But it was too early for gourmet diners. There was no one around.

She struggled, but her assailant was stronger. Something was thrown over her face—a foul-smelling blanket? Her arms were held tightly against her sides. She could hardly breathe. She felt herself being dragged.

Her continued struggles gained her nothing but ex-. haustion. This couldn't be happening!

And then they stopped. She was roughly tossed onto the ground. She hit something firm but pliant.

The blanket was lifted from her face.

"In case you thought your dear husband was going to rescue you," said a high-pitched voice that was clearly disguised, "Think again."

On the ground beside her, unconscious, was Jordan. Behind her, the voice began to laugh.

Chapter Fifteen

The blanket was thrust once again over Sara's face. "Move," said the voice. It was steel-edged now, but still high-pitched.

But Sara's only movement was to kneel. She thrust the blanket back and looked again at Jordan. He was lying so still on the bare earth of the wind-swept mountaintop. She felt his neck. Thank heavens! There was a pulse. "Jordan," she whispered frantically. "Wake up." *Please be all right,* she prayed silently. *If you have to leave me and go home to Texas, it's all right. Just don't die.*

Whether or not it was wise, even if they had no future together, she loved him.

But he didn't stir.

Sara felt a nudge at her side. It was the killer's foot. Sara turned to look up to face her assailant, but she was shoved hard to the unyielding ground and the blanket was thrown over her face yet again. "I said move!" the voice demanded.

"Where?" Sara's wrist ached from the way she landed. She rubbed it and tried to keep her temper in check. "And how am I supposed to figure out where to go with something over my head?"

"I'll lead you. Now, stand up."

Sara was reluctant to leave Jordan's side. Nevertheless, she obeyed. "Are you going to kill us?"

The voice laughed cunningly. "What do you think?"

Sara stood uncertainly. Which way was the restaurant? The car? The cliff? She couldn't tell with the blanket over her. It stank of...of what? Chemicals, she thought. And dead things.

A breeze was blowing. It rippled the leaves of the trees overhead. But there was another sound that Sara heard, very faintly. Still, it made her skin crawl.

"Then why this stupid blanket?" she demanded. "What difference does it make if I know who you are?"

"Who do you think I am?" The voice sounded smug, as if Sara would never guess. And for the moment, she wasn't certain.

"You're obviously not Dwayne Gould," she said.

"Obviously," the killer agreed.

"But you're in law enforcement." Sara had to keep him—her?—talking. Backup was on the way. If she were diligent enough...

"You're right. And by the way, I've already made sure that no one comes up here to help you. I've called off any backup you might have arranged. I have one of those handy little computer systems, too, you know. How do you think I lured you up here? I pretended to be your dear husband."

Sara felt as though all her hopes had been knocked as unconscious as Jordan.

Jordan. He had come here to help her family, because he had cared for Stu—never mind whether he cared for her. His values as a Texas Ranger required that he not ignore someone in need of his services. Her father had asked for help that went far beyond any duty Jordan might have felt toward Stu.

He had married her.

And now, she couldn't let him die because of it.

There was a sound to Sara's right, like a phone ringing in the distance. Perhaps it was from inside the restaurant. But if she called out or tried to run in that direction, she might be dead before anyone there could help. And if someone tried, the Good Samaritan might die, as well.

Not to mention Jordan.

"Tell me who you think I am," the murderer demanded. "I'll give you a hint. You see me a lot, Sara, on the job."

Sara guessed that part of the criminal's thrill was to watch how well everyone else had been fooled. "Well, if you're in law enforcement and you've got one of the computers, you could be a cop." She thought a moment. Who did she see a lot?

"Ramon?"

"Aren't you the sexist?" The strangely shrill voice laughed. "Who said I was a man? A woman can be a killer, too. Don't you know that?"

Sara had believed that all along. But if it were a uniform cop she saw a lot of, and it wasn't Ramon... Shocked, she asked, "June?"

"Maybe. Now let's get going." Her arm was seized roughly and she was steered in a direction she thought was away from the restaurant.

June? The killer hadn't denied it, but...

"I don't believe you're June at all," Sara said.

"Why not? You probably don't remember, but Stu and June were dating. They had a lover's quarrel not long before Stu died. Maybe that was the reason he was killed.''

Sara shook her head beneath the confining, smothering blanket. ''No. June has been my friend. I would know it if she were the killer.''

That sound again: like keys jingling. And it was growing louder. Why did it grate on her so?

They stopped moving. Sara was shoved forward. Her shin hit something hard. ''Step up into the car,'' piped the voice from behind her.

''All right.'' Why did the sound of rattling keys so upset Sara? She felt with her hands, then stepped into a car. Which one was it? she wondered as the door slammed shut behind her. She was in the passenger seat; she could feel the dashboard in front of her.

The rattling noise was a little more distant now. Did that mean her assailant was moving away? Maybe she—no, it couldn't be June!—he was going to get Jordan. Slowly, Sara reached toward her left. Yes! There was a computer. But could she turn it on without seeing? She lifted the blanket just a little. There was the microphone, hanging on the dashboard! Stealthily, she picked it up, pushed the button and called quietly into it, ''Code Thirty! Officer needs assistance. Emergency! Repeat, Code Thirty. Emergency! This is Dispatcher Sara Shepard Dawes. I—''

She heard something outside, stopped talking and replaced the microphone. She would have to rely on Izzy's knowledge of where she'd gone, plus the sophisticated computer system, to reveal their location to the backup that now, certainly, would come.

But when? Would it be too late?

She heard something to her left; the car door opening. ''Your husband is damned heavy,'' huffed the killer's high voice, sounding out of breath. "I had to drag him all the way over here."

That was why she hadn't been caught using the microphone; the killer had been too distracted.

Jordan was still unconscious, if he were being dragged. He had to be all right....

But neither one of them would be all right if Sara didn't do something quickly. Before it was too late.

"I don't think you're June at all," she said. "June is a police officer. She takes continuous training in martial arts and life-saving techniques. Even though she's a woman, she'd be strong enough to get Jordan over here relatively easily."

"You're right. Guess again."

Oh, Lord. She was playing guessing games with a madman—for now she was convinced it was a man.

"Ramon," she blurted.

"Of course," said the voice. "I did, after all, argue with Stu about the way he treated my partner June."

But it couldn't be Ramon, or her captor wouldn't have admitted it so readily. He was leading up to some big revelation. Sara could feel it.

Jordan's pet suspect had been Carroll Heumann. The acting police chief had shown up at all the crime scenes and bullied everyone. Was that so he could be sure no evidence arose against him? He had enough clout and knowledge to have gotten evidence together to plant at Dwayne's, even body parts.

Still, Sara doubted it was him. But she said anyway, "No, I don't believe you're Ramon. Chief Heumann?"

The killer cackled in glee. "You've guessed it this time. That's me." But the voice remained falsetto. If Sara had been right, there would have been no reason for him to continue to disguise his voice. And Heumann also would have taken continued training. Even though he was overweight, he would probably have been able to lift Jordan, at least in a fireman's carry.

She felt the seat shift downward beside her. Someone was in the driver's seat—Jordan?

She reached out. She felt him slump over so that his head was heavy on her shoulder. She cradled it against her, wishing she could kiss him—wishing she could remove the blanket.

"Dammit!" cried the killer. "Sit up, you son of a—" The key jingling began again, as if in agitation.

Suddenly Sara sucked in a breath. She wanted to scream. She wanted to lunge out of the car, do something. Immediately.

She finally remembered where she had heard that sound before.

In the hotel room.

She had gone down in the elevator with her father to the room they had rented to get dressed in. He hadn't felt well. Something had upset his stomach and he had needed his antacid pills.

Dr. Lloyd Pederzani, the medical examiner, had shown up in the room while Sara had been in the bathroom getting her father a glass of water.

"YOU!" her father exclaimed. "Lloyd? But why?"

Sara stayed where she was, but peeked into the hotel room.

Lloyd was there with her father. Upstairs, at the wedding, he had been dressed in a tuxedo, as were all the other men. Now, he had thrown a green medical gown over it, pulled on latex gloves, and placed a surgical cap over his hair. Oddly, she noticed that his hands were in his pockets; he was rattling his keys, louder and louder. His gaunt face was almost skeletal as he gave a rictus of a smile.

"Stu was getting too close," he answered in a calm, soothingly falsetto voice. "He knew I was the only one who could have done it. He came to see me, to ask questions. He pretended he had another suspect and just wanted my opinion. But I knew. So I killed him. I took him by surprise by injecting him first to knock him out before I stabbed him. Since I did the autopsy myself, no one ever found out.

"But he must have left you something for you to have gotten so close again. And for Sara to have married a Texas Ranger—too dangerous. I'll have to take care of him, too—later. Right now, well, that medication I put in your drink to upset your stomach won't kill you—but this will."

He pulled out a sheathed steak knife, bared it and lunged at her father. But he apparently didn't know that Sara was in the bathroom. She charged out, startling Lloyd as he stabbed her father—but with surprising strength, he flung her against the wall. Her head struck it—hard. Excruciating pain shot through her before she lost consciousness.

SHE HAD FORGOTTEN everything—until now.

But what should she do about it?

She turned in the seat, surreptitiously using the blanket to cover the dashboard. Carefully, she reached around beneath it and pushed the microphone button, locking it in the hands-free position. She hoped it was set to broadcast on multiple frequencies. Maybe someone, even a cop in a neighboring town, would hear it and send help.

"All right, Lloyd," she said in a conversational but

slightly raised voice. "My memory has finally returned." She pushed the blanket off her face, being careful to keep it draped over the dashboard and the open mike. "There's really no need for this any longer."

"No, dear Sara, I guess there isn't." His voice had returned to normal, and it sounded sad. In the dim overhead light from his still-open door, she couldn't help but notice that he *looked* sad, too. Holding a 9 mm gun trained on her, he was leaning over Jordan's still, pale body.

Oh, Jordan... What was wrong with him? Had he been injected with something to knock him out—or worse? She had to get him to a hospital right away. What if he were dying?

What if he was already dead?

She had to think of something.

"I'd really wished there was some other way than to kill you," Lloyd was saying. "I'd hoped your amnesia would be permanent. But then you started to remember small things. I suspected it was a matter of time."

Keep him talking, Sara told herself. Help would arrive.

If only they did it quietly, without sirens or lights. But she'd had no opportunity to give such instructions.

"It was easy for you to plant things in Dwayne's apartment, wasn't it?"

"Yes. I'll miss him, too. But better that he get imprisoned or executed than me."

"You sent the note to Ramon—didn't you?—to make me suspicious that Jordan killed my father after arguing with him."

"Too bad you didn't buy it," Lloyd said sadly. "I wanted to divide and conquer."

"But Jordan couldn't have been the serial killer. He had just moved here."

"That's true. But he could have done some copycat killings to hide his murder of Casper. That's what I'd hoped people would believe."

But they hadn't, Sara knew. She continued, hoping Lloyd wouldn't cease his conversation to get down to his evil business. "What about the note to me at the apartment murder scene, and all the other things that happened there? Did you set them up?"

Lloyd's smirk, with his skeletal face, appeared ghastly. "Weren't they spectacular? I wanted to scare you. It made the game more fun. That's why the phone calls and messages, too. And at the apartment, I particularly liked the touch of the exploding car, didn't you? Such a great distraction. I made sure all the evidence there would point to Dwayne."

"You hired those kids to lure Jordan off with the gasoline can, and me with the fake murder weapon, didn't you?" Sara was quivering with nervousness. Was anyone listening?

When would the backup arrive?

"Certainly, but that actually was the murder weapon. The young man I hired—while I was disguised, naturally—didn't know that, of course. And now I have it hidden safely away—till next time, perhaps."

"But why, Lloyd? Why did you kill all those people?"

He shrugged. "At first, I just wanted to make sure there was enough work to justify the existence of an independent medical examiner's office in this small town... Then I discovered how much I enjoyed fooling everyone.

"I knew enough about how to prevent leaving physical evidence such as hair, body fluids, fingerprints and the like— Even if I fouled up, I'd be able to attribute any item to a techie picking something up I'd left after the scene to declare the victim dead.

"I saved the bloody gowns, caps, gloves and masks... In fact, I've so much plantable evidence left to convict Dwayne, I'll become a hero. I'll even get the police chief's job instead of that idiot Heumann— But enough of this idle chatter." His expression turned hard. "It's time for your dear hubby and you to die."

"If you kill Jordan and me, everyone will know Dwayne's innocent."

That horrible death's head smile appeared on Lloyd's too thin face once more. "Not at all. I'm too smart for that. Your deaths will appear to be accidental. So sad for such happy young newlyweds, to have their futures cut short like that." He laughed.

He was insane, Sara thought. But of course he had to be, to have killed so many people, and so viciously.

He moved the gun so that it was aimed right at Jordan. Lloyd reached down and touched his neck. "Your husband is still alive, you know. If you don't do just as I say, I'll shoot him right now."

Desperately, Sara grasped for a way to save at least Jordan's life. If she did what Lloyd said, they would both die, anyway, unless help arrived in time. Maybe she could just focus his attention on her.

Jordan couldn't die. She wouldn't let him.

"You know, Lloyd," she said, "you're using the wrong leverage here."

He frowned. "What do you mean?"

"You don't know the true story of my marriage to Jordan. That's where you've made your mistake."

"Mistake? I never make mistakes."

Sara made herself laugh. "You did this time. I'd certainly be sorry to see Jordan die. He's a very nice man. But it was my father's idea that we marry. As you know, Jordan's a Texas Ranger. Dad figured that if he simply showed up here one day, the serial killer we were chasing would know Jordan had come to nab him. We knew the killer was smart and was affiliated with Santa Gregoria law enforcement. Dad had only recently found Stu's evidence to that effect."

"Then...then you married this man to keep me from becoming suspicious?" Lloyd's voice raised in outrage. "That whole damned wedding was staged? But Reverend Watt married you. Was he in on it?"

"It was a genuine wedding," Sara said. "But not for the usual reasons, like love and commitment. We fooled you, didn't we? And I really don't care if you kill Jordan."

He was breathing so hard that his gun hand shook, but he pointed the weapon toward Sara. "It doesn't matter," he said from between clenched teeth. "You'll both die. I'm especially not going to take any chances that this Texas Ranger will survive." He moved the gun so that it was again aimed at Jordan.

Damn! Sara thought. If she was any judge, he was ready to pull the trigger.

"I was going to send you both over the cliff in the car, but I'll turn this into a murder suicide instead. Yes, that's it. I'll say that you actually did love him but he was ready to leave now that the murderer—Dwayne—had been caught."

Sara nearly flinched at how close Lloyd was to the truth. But she couldn't let him shoot Jordan.

"This is Jordan's gun, after all," Lloyd continued. "I took it after I injected him with something to make him sleep for a while. But of course now he'll never wake up."

"The thing is..." Sara said hastily, surreptitiously reaching for the door handle. "You won't be able to tell anyone anything. Or at least, nothing they'll believe. If you'll look at the microphone under this stupid blanket, you'll see that it's been turned on. With luck, it's been broadcasting in several frequencies. Law enforcement officers all over Central California now know that you're the killer."

His face turned purple in the pale overhead light. His eyes were huge and furious. His gun hand raised—just as Sara shoved open her door. "You damned b—"

The gun went off. Her ears ringing, Sara ducked and rolled out instinctively, even as she heard the bullet thunk into the roof of the car. How had the shot gone so wild in so confined a space?

She looked up—and there was Jordan. Though he looked awful, he had grabbed Lloyd's gun hand. Another shot rang out. "Get out of here, Sara," Jordan rasped, his voice faint.

He was weak. He wouldn't be able to hold Lloyd—who had the strength of a madman—off for very long.

"Oh, I don't think so," she said.

"Dammit, Sara, if you're ever going to listen, now's the time." Jordan was panting. He had somehow wrestled Lloyd out the driver's door and onto the ground.

Sara moved from her side of the car and crawled around the front to the other side. Lloyd was on top of Jordan. Jordan was struggling to keep the gun from being pointed at him. She knew he wouldn't be able to hold out much longer. She had to find something—anything—to use as a weapon. But there was nothing within her reach.

Her only recourse was to become the target. She looked up at the sky for a moment. The stars were out in infinite numbers. She might never again see them. A cool mountain breeze blew through her hair. Would this be the last time she would experience wind and weather?

No matter. Jordan would live. He was still managing to keep the gun from being pointed directly at him, but he was quickly losing the battle. No more time. She had to do something immediately.

She yelled tauntingly, "You'll only get one of us, Lloyd."

That distracted him for a moment. He looked at her briefly, but long enough for Jordan to land a glancing blow on Lloyd's jaw. In moments, Jordan was on top. He finally had control of the gun.

"It's over, Pederzani," he said, gasping for breath. Then, "Sara, can you come over here? I need a little help." He managed to tell her where to find his handcuffs. She snapped them on Lloyd's wrists just as the first of the police cars, lights blazing and sirens blaring, arrived in the parking lot.

"Take the gun, Sara, and hold it on him," Jordan said. He looked ghastly white in the headlights. She wanted to bend and kiss him, make certain he was all right. But Lloyd was on his knees, trying to rise, probably to run away.

Sara took the gun from Jordan, assumed the stance she had learned on the firing range, and said, "Freeze, Lloyd," just as Jordan folded into a heap on the ground beside her.

Chapter Sixteen

Jordan cracked open his eyes. His hospital room was nearly identical to the Spartan white facility in which Sara had spent the night of their wedding. Not surprisingly, it smelled of overperfumed disinfectant.

His head hurt. It must have hit the ground when he'd fallen the first time, or maybe the pain was caused by the drug Pederzani had injected. He wondered if Sara had felt so miserable when she'd been thrown against the wall in the hotel room.

That caused him to open his eyes fully and sit up. Sara. Her memory had finally returned and—

"You're awake." Was he dreaming her sweet, melodic voice? He managed to turn his head without it falling off, though it felt ready to.

There she was, sitting on the straight-backed chair beside the bed. Her black hair was combed back from her beautiful face, and there were dark circles beneath her drooping hazel eyes. She was wearing a clean white T-shirt that read Property Of SGPD, showing her bust-line to full advantage, and snug blue jeans.

She had never looked lovelier. He wanted to drag her down onto the bed and touch her all over.

Later, he told himself. When there wasn't the risk of

some nosy nurse bursting in. Besides, he'd be able to make them both feel even better when his damned headache was gone.

"Sure, I'm awake. But you shouldn't be. You look like you haven't slept in days."

"For one day," she admitted with half a smile. "You were out for a long time after they brought you in here."

"And you were with me the whole time?"

She nodded, looking embarrassed. "You got into this whole mess because of my family. I wanted to make sure you were okay."

And that was the only reason why she'd been here?

Why should he have expected otherwise? Except—

Except that he now knew that he loved her. But she hadn't married him for love. She still didn't care that way for him—did she?

"Sara..." he began, wishing his head didn't hurt so badly. There was a lot he wanted to say, but he wasn't sure he could phrase it all right with his mind so muddled.

"I'll bet you want to know what's gone on in the past day or so," she said. She frowned then, her lovely dark brows puckering. He wanted to reach out to smooth them, to take away whatever was bothering her. He did, in fact, reach toward her and she took his hand. Hers was warm and soft, and he managed to lace his fingers with hers. "Do you remember what happened, Jordan?" she asked.

"What happened?" For a moment he didn't know what she was talking about.

"Behind the restaurant. With Lloyd." She appeared a little frantic. "Jordan, you didn't lose *your* memory from the drug or the bump on your head, did you?"

He blinked and forbade himself from smiling. "Just who is such a pretty lady who's come to my bedside to hold my hand? Are you by any chance an angel?"

"Go to the devil, Jordan Dawes!" she said, swatting him gently on the left shoulder, obviously careful to not affect the IV in his arm.

"So that's who I am?"

"As if you didn't know. You knew who *I* was when you woke up, so you've got to know who *you* are."

"Is that how it works?"

"Uh-huh." She nodded her head decisively, but her lips twitched as though she, too, were fighting a smile.

"Okay, then, I'm Jordan Dawes and you're Sara Shepard Dawes, and together we caught a serial killer, right?"

"Your memory is working just fine, Ranger."

Ranger. That word certainly triggered memories for him, not that he had actually forgotten. But now that their mission had reached a successful conclusion, he would have to leave.

Unless—

"How are you feeling, Sara?" he asked. "Have you gotten your memory completely back now?"

"Mostly, though there are still some gaps. Most notably, I don't remember much on the day Lloyd killed Dad and hurt me before the time we were in the hotel room."

"Then you don't remember our wedding?"

She shook her head. "Not that it matters," she said, smiling ruefully.

She was right, of course. Then why did he feel as though he had been pierced by one of Pederzani's damned steak knives?

Pederzani. Jordan hadn't been able to direct the collection of evidence against him. Was everything going well?

"Tell me just what's gone on since I've been unconscious, Sara. Has evidence against Lloyd been found?"

"Plenty of it. It seems that our dedicated medical examiner is one of those serial killers who enjoys keeping souvenirs. Among other things, the knife from the apartment murder was in his possession—the one the young man at the scene lured me away with. He, of course, just thought he was being paid to participate in a practical joke. Some of Lloyd's other souvenirs consisted of body parts that he took while the bodies of those he'd murdered were in his autopsy lab."

"Delightful. So the finger..."

Sara's face paled. Jordan didn't want to continue, but she took up the rest of his sentence. "The finger that Lloyd purported to be Stu's wasn't actually his. He thought that if we tested it faster and thought there was some new killer on the loose, we'd get confused, allowing the trail to him to grow even colder."

"Strange reasoning," Jordan said, shaking his head. Mistake. He winced at the pain.

"Can I get you anything?" Sara stood beside him in an instant. Her fingertips smoothed back his hair from his forehead near the bandage on his head, and he closed his eyes, reveling in the feel of her soft strokes. "Does this make it feel worse?" she asked.

"Not at all. Please don't stop." He smiled into her concerned hazel eyes, then grew serious again. "Where was the evidence found? At Lloyd's home?"

Sara shook her head. "He was much more brazen than that. He had a locked office at the morgue with file cabinets—and even a freezer."

"He must have known he'd get caught someday," Jordan said. "Has he confessed?"

"In a way. Of course he was read his Miranda rights, so everything should be admissible. He thinks himself too smart to need a lawyer, but from what I gather he's said he only killed when he was bored, to liven up the medical examiner's office and perplex his co-workers in law enforcement."

"What!" Jordan exclaimed. "That was his reason? What a nasty, crazy…no. We don't want him to get off on a successful insanity plea. He's not crazy, just crafty."

"That's for sure," Sara said.

She sat on the edge of Jordan's bed. Her curvaceous derriere was only inches from his body. He remembered what it felt like to caress it…. Oh, yes, his memory was just fine. So was his body; he shifted a little as he felt himself growing hard.

"Do you know how he chose his victims?" she asked, bringing his thoughts reluctantly back to the matter at hand.

"No," he said. "Did he actually explain that, too?"

"That's what I've heard, though Carroll Heumann is hardly about to let a lowly dispatcher sit in on the interrogation."

"Even when that dispatcher was one of the people who caught the murderer? Never mind. What did you hear?"

"That he purposely chose people carefully so they would appear random, different backgrounds and settings and all, to make it even tougher to figure out what he was doing. But he wanted everyone to know it was the same brilliant killer, so he used common steak knives as his signature—since the bodies became 'dead meat.'"

Jordan wished he had Lloyd Pederzani's scrawny body in front of him right about then. He'd show him "dead meat."

But he knew himself better than that. He was a Texas Ranger, as well as a detective in the Santa Gregoria Police Department. He would let the law take care of Lloyd Pederzani.

Though when he got out of this hole of a hospital, he'd make certain that the case built against the medical examiner was air-tight. He wouldn't escape on a technicality. Not this cold-blooded murderer.

"Jordan, are you all right?"

"What?"

"You looked as if you were thousands of miles away," Sara said. She smiled slightly, though it didn't seem to reach her eyes. "Back in Texas already?"

"Not yet," he said. "But soon."

Too soon, he thought. For whenever he left Sara, it would be too soon.

"Good," she said brightly, slipping off his bed. She stood beside him. "I think it's about time for both of us to move on with our lives, don't you? I'll be back to see you later." And then she walked out of the room.

Jordan stared after her, then drove his fist hard against the firm hospital mattress. Why did it feel as if she were walking out on him, rather than simply moving on?

SARA'S LIFE— What would it be now? she wondered.

She didn't have much time to dwell on it as she took over the dispatch desk from Izzy at the start of her day shift. She'd managed to get a substitute the previous day, so she could stay with Jordan in the hospital.

She'd had to be certain he was all right.

And now that he was…?

She was thrilled that the doctors said there would be no nasty lingering side effects from the drug that Lloyd had injected, or from the blow to Jordan's head when he'd fallen. His memory was fine. His headaches, though severe for now, would go away.

And so would he….

She couldn't dwell on that now.

In between computer messages and phone calls, she made a couple of calls of her own. Both were hard.

Both were necessary.

At the end of her shift, she went home to the house she had once shared with her family, and then with Jordan, and went to bed. Alone. Lonely. And knowing that this was the way things would likely be for a very long time.

JORDAN'S HEAD was much better when Sara came to visit him the next morning. His mood wasn't.

"They're letting me out of here later today," he said. "At last. I was starting to go stir crazy."

"That's great," Sara said. She was in uniform, obviously ready to return to the station for her next dispatching shift. Though he liked her better in a T-shirt and jeans, and preferred her in nothing at all, she filled out the uniform in all the right places. Jordan wanted her in his arms.

But once again, her smile seemed just a little too forced. "I have some news for you," she continued. "I made a couple of phone calls you'll be interested in."

"Really? What?" What he was most interested in was taking out the nasty IV and getting Sara into his arms.

"I called your office in Houston. I spoke with a Captain Frederington, who said he was your boss, and that he's happy to hear that your leave of absence will be over soon. He's eager to get you back."

"Great." Why didn't it make Jordan ecstatic to hear that ol' Milt Frederington might actually have acknowledged missing him? The guy was a tough, though fair, taskmaster who rarely showed appreciation.

Sara suddenly found something on a tray near his bed that she apparently thought needed to be straightened. She turned her back on him.

"I also called an old family friend. He's a lawyer, and he's promised to handle our annulment quickly and cleanly. I told him to start drawing up the papers. There wouldn't be any dispute about property division or anything like that. Right?" She finally turned to face him. Her eyes looked troubled. Did she really think he'd try to gain anything out of this situation?

"Right," he said gruffly. "Thanks for getting it started."

LATER THAT DAY Jordan checked himself out of the hospital without waiting for Sara's shift to be over. He returned to the Shepard house and went to his bedroom—the room that had once been Stu's.

"We got him, old buddy," Jordan said, looking at the framed photograph on the dresser of his friend before he'd known him. He was holding a high school football trophy. Jordan had found the photograph in Casper's bedroom a while back. Somehow, he thought Stu knew what had happened—Casper, too.

Jordan considered packing his things. No, he'd have to go into the station tomorrow to make sure the case against Pederzani was flawless. He would stay however long it took to be certain, and then he could leave.

Still, he would get back to Texas just as soon as possible. It was what he'd always planned. Except—

Except he hadn't planned falling in love with Sara.

She'd made it clear, though, that she was ready to end their sham of a marriage now.

And the job he loved as a Texas Ranger was waiting for him.

No decision needed to be made, right?

Maybe.

There was, however, one loose end that he might be able to tie up. And it might just lead to the tying up of yet another.

He went downstairs to the kitchen, lifted the phone receiver off the wall, and made a call.

SARA DROVE HOME alone after her shift. Jordan hadn't come to get her.

Not that she was surprised. But she had called the hospital and learned that he had checked himself out. Where was he now?

Surely he wouldn't have left without saying good-bye.

After learning he'd been released, she'd half expected him to show up at the station to find out first-hand how the case against Lloyd was shaping up. But though she'd watched and listened for him, he hadn't appeared.

Well, there was no use worrying about him. At least he should no longer be in any danger.

It certainly made her feel relieved to know that no one was after her any longer.

And poor Dwayne Gould had assuredly been thrilled to be released, though he hadn't been happy to learn that the boss who'd been his ostensible friend and mentor had tried to frame him.

She pulled onto her street, then into the driveway of her pretty gray stucco house, with all the brightly colored flowers in front. The house she now remembered growing up in.

The house she would soon live in all alone, for the first time ever.

"Stop feeling sorry for yourself," she reprimanded herself. She would be fine.

But she was pleased to see Jordan's white Mustang parked by the curb. At least he hadn't left yet.

When she let herself inside the front door, she called, "Jordan? Are you here?"

"Be down in a second," came a voice from upstairs.

She smiled. She was going to see him again soon. But the smile was bittersweet, and she sighed deeply.

She was going to miss seeing him every day.

She forbore from stomping her foot at herself. Instead, she went into the kitchen and poured herself a glass of ice water. The coolness felt good going down her throat. She'd done a lot of talking that day, both to investigators and on the microphone. Her fingers had been busy, too, on the dispatch computer.

It had been a long, though rewarding, day.

Jordan came into the kitchen. He wore a blue denim shirt open at the neck, revealing a little of his light chest hair. Sara sighed. She would miss this handsome, sexy man.

"How are you feeling?" she asked.

"The headache's now down to a dull throb. And you?"

"I'm fine," she said. "Perfect."

"You certainly are." His deep, deep blue eyes scanned her from head to toe, and she felt herself flush.

"Hope you don't look that way at everyone in a police uniform," she said.

"Hardly. But why don't you change clothes? I want to take you out to a celebratory dinner."

"Sure." Not that she felt much like celebrating the end of their relationship. But that would be part of it, too.

Still, she took her time and dressed in a pretty outfit with a black silk, scoop neck blouse and a long black skirt. She fastened on a marcasite choker that had been her mother's and put on high heels.

Jordan whistled as she came downstairs. "We'll have to celebrate more often."

Of course, Sara thought grimly. *You can celebrate in Texas, and I'll celebrate right here.*

But he'd changed clothes, too. He was in a dark suit that showed off the breadth of his shoulders and the taper of his waist. He looked wonderful.

She was really going to miss him.

"You're beautiful, Sara," he said, coming toward her. She still stood on the bottom step. "I'm glad you're not in uniform now, since I have something to say to you, and it has nothing to do with either of us being in law enforcement."

"What's that?" Her mouth had suddenly gone dry.

"Do you remember when I proposed to you the first time?" He took her hand and led her into the living room. There, he motioned for her to sit on the formal café-au-lait-colored sofa.

"Not really. I thought *Dad* proposed to *you*." And then his words struck her. The *first* time? She began trembling. She had to have misunderstood.

He laughed. "Sort of. But half in jest, I got down on my knees like this, in front of both of you, and took your hand." He knelt on the floor and put out his hand. She slipped her fingers into it. She got it. He was just helping her to remember. That was all.

But she couldn't quite still her hand in his. He grasped it tighter.

"The thing is, Sara, I was kidding then. Right now, I'm serious. Will you marry me?"

She swallowed, staring into his eyes. They watched hers, and she saw a vulnerability in them. He *was* serious!

"I—"

"I guess I'm not doing this well, forgetting to say things in the order I should."

"Forgetting is my department." But Sara's voice came out in a whisper.

Jordan smiled at her. "Okay. First, I spoke with Mayor Casey. She's not happy with the way Acting Police Chief Heumann has been doing the job. He's been doing more politicking for the position than actual work as police chief. She's offered the position to me."

Sara couldn't believe her ears. "And…and did you take it?"

"I asked her to give me until tomorrow to decide. And my decision is based upon your answer."

"My answer?"

"Yes, but wait just one more moment. The last time, we got married for expediency, to catch a killer. This time, I want us to get married for love…because I do love you, Sara. I think maybe I fell for you when you were that little kid who was so eager to make an impression on her big brother's friend.''

"I know that's when I fell in love with you." Sara felt tears rolling down her cheeks. Jordan reached up with his free hand and gently wiped them away with his thumb.

"Then marry me for real, Sara."

"We *are* married," she said with a small laugh. "Remember? Dad insisted that it be a real wedding to fool the killer."

"True, but you don't remember it, and it wasn't for the right reasons. Let's get married again, or at least renew our vows, for the right reasons, okay?"

"Okay!" Sara tugged Jordan's hand so he joined her on the sofa.

After a long kiss he said, "And this time, we'll videotape the ceremony. I don't want you ever to be able to say again that you don't remember marrying me."

Sara laughed, then kissed him again. "I'll never forget," she said.

Psst...

HARLEQUIN®
INTRIGUE®

has an even *bigger* secret—

but it's **confidential**

till September 2001!

HARLEQUIN®
INTRIGUE®
and HARPER ALLEN present

THE AVENGERS

Bound by the ties they forged as soldiers
of fortune, these agents fearlessly put their
lives on the line for a worthy cause.
But now they're about to face their
greatest challenge—love!

August 2001
GUARDING JANE DOE

September 2001
SULLIVAN'S LAST STAND

Available at your favorite retail outlet.

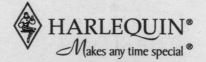

HARLEQUIN®
Makes any time special®

Visit us at www.eHarlequin.com　　HIAVENGERS

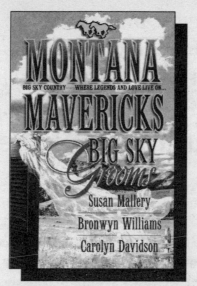

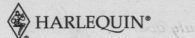
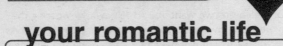

Harlequin truly does make any time special. ... This year we are celebrating weddings in style!

To help us celebrate, we want you to tell us how wearing the Harlequin wedding gown will make your wedding day special. As the grand prize, Harlequin will offer one lucky bride the chance to **"Walk Down the Aisle"** in the Harlequin wedding gown!

There's more...

For her honeymoon, she and her groom will spend five nights at the **Hyatt Regency Maui.** As part of this five-night honeymoon at the hotel renowned for its romantic attractions, the couple will enjoy a candlelit dinner for two in Swan Court, a sunset sail on the hotel's catamaran, and duet spa treatments.

To enter, please write, in, 250 words or less, how wearing the Harlequin wedding gown will make your wedding day special. The entry will be judged based on its emotionally compelling nature, its originality and creativity, and its sincerity. This contest is open to Canadian and U.S. residents only and to those who are 18 years of age and older. There is no purchase necessary to enter. Void where prohibited. See further contest rules attached. Please send your entry to:

Walk Down the Aisle Contest

In Canada	In U.S.A.
P.O. Box 637	P.O. Box 9076
Fort Erie, Ontario	3010 Walden Ave.
L2A 5X3	Buffalo, NY 14269-9076

You can also enter by visiting www.eHarlequin.com

Win the Harlequin wedding gown and the vacation of a lifetime!
The deadline for entries is October 1, 2001.

New York Times bestselling authors

DEBBIE MACOMBER
JAYNE ANN KRENTZ
HEATHER GRAHAM &
TESS GERRITSEN

lead

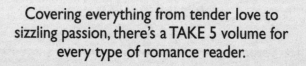

Covering everything from tender love to
sizzling passion, there's a TAKE 5 volume for
every type of romance reader.

Plus

With $5.00 worth of coupons inside each volume,
this is one deal you shouldn't miss!

Look for it in August 2001.

HARLEQUIN®
INTRIGUE®

43 *Light St.*

has been *the* address for outstanding romantic suspense for more than a decade! Now REBECCA YORK* blasts the hinges off the front door with a new trilogy— MINE TO KEEP.

Look for these great stories on the corner of heart-stopping romance and breathtaking suspense!

THE MAN FROM TEXAS
August 2001

NEVER ALONE
October 2001

LASSITER'S LAW
December 2001

COME ON OVER... WE'LL KEEP THE LIGHTS ON.

Available at your favorite retail outlet.

*Ruth Glick writing as Rebecca York

HARLEQUIN®
*M*akes any time special ®

Visit us at www.eHarlequin.com

HILIGHTST